UTAH SUMMER

**Center Point
Large Print**

**This Large Print Book carries the
Seal of Approval of N.A.V.H.**

UTAH SUMMER

Lauran Paine

CENTER POINT PUBLISHING
THORNDIKE, MAINE

This Center Point Large Print edition
is published in the year 2007 by arrangement with
Golden West Literary Agency.

Copyright © 2007 by Lauran Paine in the U.S.
Originally published under the pseudonym Harry Beck
in Great Britain in 1977 by Robert Hale & Company.

The text of this Large Print edition is unabridged. In other
aspects, this book may vary from the original edition. Printed in
Thailand. Set in 16-point Times New Roman type.

ISBN: 1-58547-912-8
ISBN 13: 978-1-58547-912-2

Library of Congress Cataloging-in-Publication Data

Paine, Lauran.
    Utah Summer / Lauran Paine.--Center Point large print ed.
    p. cm.
    ISBN-13: 978-1-58547-912-2 (lib. bdg. : alk. paper)
    1. Large type books. I. Title.

PS3566.A34U85 2007
813'.54--dc22

2006028368

UTAH SUMMER

Chapter One

FROM SUNDAY TO BIVOUAC

From Fort Sunday to the Painted Desert by way of Grand Canyon, following every crooked dog-leg of the Little Colorado River was a breathtakingly awesome trip. There was probably no other stretch of country on earth as unique, as color-splashed, as drunkenly up-ended, tilted, pounded flat, and as lavishly streaked with colors, not shades nor pastels, but scarlet reds and turquoise blues, mustard yellows, orange and black, and chocolaty brown where the Little Colorado ran, carrying silt from the east end of Grand Canyon.

It was also desolate. Wild and breathtaking and desolate. If the stage had come to rest, silence would have descended like an avalanche crushing the passengers, one man, one woman, one young boy, with its terrible depth of hush.

The driver and gunguard on the box, accustomed to the road and surrounded by the noise of their hitch and coach, and their occasional conversation, rode along unaware of the stillness, but completely aware of the emptiness.

Once this whole country between Fort Sunday and Bivouac had been the domain of Indian nations, none of them large, all of them dedicated from cradle to grave to struggling for existence in a country where Nature had lavished beauty and omitted productivity; some had been aggressive—like the sub-tribes of Apaches—but mostly, the tribesmen had been very primitive, barely able to maintain themselves, simple, and not very concerned with what was happening along the perimeters of their big-sky country.

Now, they were gone. All but hidden pockets of holdouts who hid by day and foraged by night like desperadoes, in their own god-forsaken huge and awesome emptiness. There was a decimated small band, for example, who lived at the bottom of Grand Canyon, around a blue-water pond, where they had camouflaged brush-shelters and scratched in the hard soil to plant crops of maize and squash, and otherwise hunted the stunted deer of their sterile, hidden world, while above them stages rocketed past daily, scarcely visible except for the dust they jerked to life and left suspended in the still air.

The country changed from Grand Canyon northward, and the closer coach-passengers got to Bivouac, which lay northward from the Arizona-Utah line, over in the direction of the San Juan River to the east, the more grass there was, more trees, pines and piñons, and the more productive the land became. Also, there were mountains. They were visible all the time coach-passengers were crossing upcountry from Fort Sunday. First, as heat-hazed distant dark slopes and upthrusts, then, as the miles fell rearward, they became less dreamlike and more massively solid and forbidding, and finally, by the time the stage had skirted around through the northward parklands out of the desert and towards the rolling grasslands, the mountains became the source and the substance of everything, and the empty desert, left behind, assumed the dreamlike quality, shimmering back down there with its unearthly silence, its limitless vast emptiness, unreal because of its magnificent beauty, and its complete malevolence.

There were only two times of the year the run between Sunday and Bivouac could be made without sweltering discomfort. Early spring and late autumn. Otherwise, even the natives—Indians and Mexicans—who were pigmented for it, avoided the heat, which was insufferable, and the desert sunlight, which was downright deadly.

During the hot time of the year stages made the run at night. During daylight that immense vacuum was left entirely as it had been since The Beginning—undisturbed, unconquerable, malevolently deadly.

But the world up around Bivouac was different, perhaps because the two rivers, the San Juan and the Colorado, which unavoidably added humidity, and whose subsurface faults fed miles of rolling grasslands where stalwart trees shed fragrance and shade, made this upland of deeper soil, amenable to the works of man.

This, the lanky man on the mid-day coach, explained to the curly-headed and dark-eyed young boy as they pitched and swayed up across the first of the foothill lowlands, was where the cow camps were, and the youth, mindful of the horrors vividly related in his penny magazines, asked if this was also where the Apaches skulked.

The man turned smiling grey eyes, and said, 'A long time ago, maybe. About the time when I was your age. But the town where we're heading—that's how it got its name of Bivouac. There was an army-camp there for about eight or ten years. It was a base for the cavalry. They hunted down Indians from up here all the way south to the Mex border. Well; the town grew up and called itself Bivouac, but the soldiers went away after the last broncos had been corralled. There hasn't been Indian trouble between the Abajo Mountains, or the Carrizos, since I can remember.'

The boy's mother used a damp cloth to cool her flushed face. She had eyes as blue as cornflowers, a complexion as rich as new cream, and she did not really look old enough to have a son twelve or four-teen years of age, which the cowman assumed was the age of her boy. She did not actually look more than about eighteen or twenty, herself. She also looked very pregnant.

The boy said, 'What does Abajo mean, mister?'

'Low,' replied the man. 'The Abajos are more hills than mountains, son.'

'And Carrizo, mister?'

'It's a kind of tough grass,' said the man, smiling.

'The Carrizos are grassy hills and mountains, with lots of trees, too, but mostly they are used along their foothills where the grazing is good.' The man raised his amused grey eyes to the woman. 'You folks are new out here?'

The woman's eyes were dark with discomfort from the heat, the swaying and pitching, but they smiled back. 'From Ohio,' she explained. 'My husband came out six months ago. To the mines up around Moab. He sent for us last month and we've been on the road ever since . . . I hope we get there soon.' She looked slightly rueful and lightly laid a hand upon her vast stomach.

The cowman's gaze lost some of its warmth, very gradually. He nodded understandingly then turned back to watching the country move past.

Moab was a poor place for a man who thought anything of his family, to bring them, especially when the woman was heavy with child. It was dirty and lawless and rude. If there was a doctor up there, he had arrived within the past year, because the last time the cowman had been in Moab all they'd had was an expanding cemetery, saloons, the mines, and a ham-fisted town constable. There was a liveryman up there, named Schultz, who also extracted teeth, but there was no doctor. At least there hadn't been last year.

Moab was beyond the Abajos, out where the land turned harsher. It was more nearly a desert than the country south of the Abajos and north of the Carrizos. When the boy's sharp dark eyes picked out flashing

11

movement, and he called to the man, pointing excitedly where a small band of fleet antelope flashed their tails in flight, the man took time to explain that in this uplands grassland country, there was much game, but back down in the desert, as well as beyond the Abajos, there was almost no game at all. Then the man said, 'This is a corner of Eden,' and smiled at the boy. 'What's your name?'

'John Leland. My paw's name is Mike. And that's my mother. Her name is Ella. It's really Eleanor, but no one calls her that. Not even my paw.'

The man leaned to watch the antelope, his coat hitching up slightly to expose the walnut-handled, leather-holstered Colt, and the boy's eyes got perfectly round. He looked swiftly at his mother. She frowned a little at him, so the boy pretended not to see the sixgun and also leaned to watch as the last antelope flicked his tail and disappeared through a flourishing tall stand of chaparral.

The man leaned back, drew forth a gold watch, opened it and studied the spidery hands, then looked across at the suffering woman. 'Not much longer, Mrs. Leland. About an hour. If you lean and look up ahead you'll see a pair of twin peaks. Bivouac's about five miles this side of them in a big park.' He replaced the watch without taking his eyes off the woman. It was none of his affair, but she would do better to lie over the night at Bivouac, then be strong for the last lap of her journey up to Moab in the morning.

He settled back and continued to watch the land.

Once, when they passed a band of greasy fat, dark red cattle, his interest quickened, and the boy, noticing this, also leaned to look out.

The cattle had a big Rocking K on their right ribs, a clean, professional-looking brand. The boy had questions about that, so the man explained. Then, when the cattle were gone and the man settled back, he said, 'They're mine. The K stands for Kandelin. I'm Frank Kandelin.' At the boy's dawning expression of admiration and respect, the man smiled. 'Well; some men mine, some tend stores, and some run cattle.'

The boy would not have his awe minimized. He had been reading penny magazines since he'd been very young and knew all about cowboys and Indians and desperadoes. 'You're a cowboy,' he exclaimed, and his mother put a disapproving look on him, which he did not notice, but the cowman did, so he answered deprecatingly. 'Well; not exactly. But I was once, years ago, and it's not a very romantic life. You work long hours, ache in every joint, eat bad food, and get rained on, blown half out of the saddle—and I've never fought an Indian nor chased a bandit. Like I said, John, some men work the mines, and some men tend the stores—and when a man's not smart enough for those things, he runs cattle.'

Frank Kandelin laughed, then, as the coach began to lose headway, he straightened on the narrow seat and leaned to glance out and around. As he settled back he said, 'We're getting close to the water-box.

13

There's a turnout up ahead a half mile or so where the stages stop to tank up the teams and rest for a short spell, before we head on down into the meadows around Bivouac.'

He was right. The coach horses dropped to a steady walk, and finally turned off where trees cast pine-scented shade around an old stone-and-mortar water trough, which was fed through a hollowed-out sapling from a seepage-spring back up the gentle slope a hundred or so yards. Here, with evidence of people stopping to rest for many years on all sides— names and dates and destinations carved into tree-trunks—the driver wheeled in off the road way and brought his hitch to a halt. Then he sang out cheerily.

'Cold water, folks, and shade for half an hour.'

Frank Kandelin alighted first, moved aside for John Leland to tumble out next, then he offered the pregnant woman his hand, and guided her over to the shade where some thoughtful traveler had hacked a bench from a downed old deadfall tree.

She gave him a quavery smile and he turned back to lend a hand with the watering of the horses, with the boy getting in everyone's way in his eagerness to be of assistance. The driver was a burly, bearded, soiled man with perpetually squinted pale eyes and a wide mouth. He exuded confidence and rough good nature. He and Kandelin exchanged a wink over the clumsiness of the lad. They understood.

The gunguard was a large, swaggering, dark man,

and although he too helped with the horses, he acted as though this were a function far beneath his professional standing.

Chapter Two

THE BIRTHING

Usually, people brought food with them on these rides, and as the gunguard and driver retired to the far side of their faded, durable old coach to share some beer and meat, Frank Kandelin leaned inside the coach to haul out his small valise. There was a bottle of whiskey in it, and some tinned tomatoes and sardines. He took them over to the woman and her son, opened the tins and passed them around. The whiskey he left in the valise out of sight.

The boy, like all boys, was voracious, but his mother smilingly declined, asking only if Frank Kandelin would re-dampen her face cloth at the waterbox. Her face was very flushed.

When he returned with the wet cloth, she raised soft eyes swimming in pain, and tried to hold a desperate smile in place as she said, 'Mister Kandelin—I don't think I can make it the rest of the way.'

Then she fainted.

Frank was a man who had come to manhood

through crises and emergencies. He was only temporarily stunned into immobility. When the woman moaned, and heavily heaved her distended body, he sank to one knee to make her comfortable, and when her son recovered and asked a breathless question, Frank said, 'Go get the driver, John. Get whatever blankets they have. Tell him to get over here.'

When the driver and gunguard came, shocked by the abruptness of this unexpected trouble, Frank did not even look around. 'You got bedrolls in the boot; unroll them and fetch me your blankets. Then one of you build a little fire.'

The burly driver echoed that, 'A fire?'

Kandelin was minimal in his explanations. 'Yeah. Gather up the tomato tins and heat spring-water in them. And don't stand there, damn it.' He looked around at the frowning gunguard. 'Take the lad for a walk up through the trees,' he said.

The gunguard hitched his shellbelt, looked around at the boy, and let his breath out, raggedly, before jerking his head. 'Come along,' he said, but the boy, terror-stricken at sight of his unconscious mother lying in pine-shade moaning, would not move.

The driver returned, stumbling over his armload of none-too-clean blankets. He went briskly to work creating a pallet; of the two stage-men, he was the quickest to understand and to react. The gunguard still stood, staring.

Frank arose, tossed aside his hat, shed his jacket, and as he rolled up his sleeves he said, 'John; take the gunguard for a walk. Son, do as I say, your mother'll be all right—but for a while she won't want you—or him—around.'

The lad's large dark eyes came up, stricken. 'Is it the baby, Mister Kandelin?'

Frank smiled a little. 'Afraid so, John.'

'But he's not supposed to come until we get up to Moab.'

The driver spoke from where he knelt making the pallet, sweat making his face glisten. 'They don't wait,' he stated very matter-of-factly. 'And you can't never tell for a fact when they're coming, neither. Son—do like Mister Kandelin says,' The driver raised his head in the gunguard's direction. 'You too, Alf. You being an unmarried man, can't be no help right now.'

The boy still did not yield. 'Mister Kandelin, she's got to have a doctor.'

None of the men would have denied that, but on the other hand this was her time, and they were still about three miles from Bivouac.

The driver said, 'Mister Kandelin's pulled his share of calves, boy. Now damn it, you and Alf go on away from here!'

It was the gunguard who finally reached for the lad's arm and pulled him away. 'They know,' he said gruffly. 'They both know what they're doing. The driver's got four kids of his own back at Fort Sunday. The other feller's a big cowman hereabouts. Like you was told, boy, he knows how to birth calves.'

17

The woman's blue eyes shot wide open. She stared in stark agony up into Frank Kandelin's bronzed, hard-set face. Tears came, silently, as the driver scuttled to fill the tins and make his little fire. He was perspiring worse than if it had been mid-summer and he was back down upon the desert. Once, after he had the fire burning, he darted to the far side of the stage and emptied the container of beer, and that helped.

Frank took Ella Leland's hands between his palms. 'You breathe deeply, and when the pains come, you bear down.' He smiled down into her eyes. 'Don't worry about anything except bearing down, then resting between pains. You'll be just fine.' He released her hands as she sank back, wilting, eyes closing, then he went to the stone trough and washed his hands and arms, wiped off sweat from forehead and chin, saw the driver watching him, and gently shook his head. The driver understood.

'It's always something,' he muttered, fanning the fire with his old hat. 'I never made this run on time in my life.'

Frank went back and knelt to ease Ella onto the pallet, then he put the cool cloth upon her face and gently patted her fisted hand. She had both eyes squeezed so tightly closed water was forced out at the corners. Her flushed look was redder and her clamped-closed soft lips formed a stubborn, harsh line. Once, when she broke and lay back, loose and gasping, she looked upwards and said, 'I'm sorry. I didn't mean—it shouldn't have happened this way.

I'm—embarrassed, Mister Kandelin.'

He stoically hid all his fears and dreads when he replied. 'Why should anyone be embarrassed about birthing new life, Mrs. Leland? And this place, on the divide with the trees and sky and clean country all around; it's better than some dirty room in a boardinghouse.'

She groped for his hand, closed small, strong fingers around and bore down with surprising strength. He could feel his stomach-muscles straining with her, could feel his strength building to an apex with her strength, then ebbing, and when she sank back panting again, he could have panted in unison with her.

The sun moved very little but it moved. Borne upon an updraft of fragrant air from the huge, far meadow down where the town lay, a musical sound rising from an anvil came very softly. Closer, a busy and unconcerned woodpecker beat his head furiously against a tree-trunk, and one of the drowsing stage horses snuffled and shifted his big shod feet.

Then Ella strangled an outcry, and over at the fire the driver sprang up staring. He knew that sound.

For Frank Kandelin the ordeal was over almost before he was prepared for it. He had a clean shirt in his valise and fumbled for it when the baby first showed. Sweat dripped from his chin, his stomach was in knots.

A calf came with forelegs foremost and outstretched, its head lying close and low. He had pulled enough calves to be entirely confident, but this was

19

not a calf, and although its position was not out of rhythm with the woman's gasping pains, Frank had never been through this before and could only surmise—and pray—the child was emerging properly.

From over by his fire the driver called sharply. 'Don't rupture the cord, Mister Kandelin. Get more of the clean shirt down under there. Mind, confound it, mind!'

Ella Leland cried sharply, making a keening, piercing wail of sound, then the baby was lying wetly upon Frank's clean shirt, and Ella fainted, her enormously distended mid-section falling in, her lungs seeming barely to flutter, briefly, until a stronger need compelled them to instinctively increase the cadence of their rising and falling.

Frank looked around. The driver was clutching his soiled old sweat-stained hat into a felt ball, and smiling. 'By gawd, you done it, Mister Kandelin. By gawd, you done it neat as a whistle.'

Frank said nothing for a moment. He had to tie off the cord and to also use a dank sleeve to squeeze sweat from his pale, intensely pinched-down face. 'Bring over the water,' he muttered, and tore off a sleeve from the clean shirt to make a rag to be used in sponging off the tiny, wrinkled, quivering baby boy.

The driver walked over with two tomato tins, leaned to set them down, and said, 'Hit it's *be*hind, Mister Kandelin. Spank it. You got to make their lungs clear up by makin' them bawl.' The driver leaned still more. 'Like this,' he said, and smartly stung the raw, red, wrinkled rump with the palm of a calloused hand large enough to cover both cheeks.

He did that twice, and the squirming baby in Frank Kandelin's arms reacted by jerking spasmodically, then twisting its wrinkled face half around to let go with a furious, harsh outcry.

The driver smiled. 'Boy,' he said. 'That's how things should be. Here, sponge him off, wrap him in the shirt, and hand him over. Then you look after the missus.'

They made a good pair. The driver had been through this several times and knew the procedures, although he would not have been very clean nor gentle about performing them. Frank knew nothing, but was clean and gentle. When he handed up the child and shook off sweat, he and the driver exchanged a look, then a smile.

Frank's body ached, his hands were unsteady, and when he rocked back, his legs and shoulders and back pained him. He inhaled deeply, exhaled, dug for the bottle of whiskey, uncorked it, took down two big swallows, then leaned to dribble some down the sweat-covered, panting woman. She coughed, swallowed, coughed again, and looked straight upwards.

'Boy,' said Frank, quietly. 'Strong as a bull, Mrs. Leland. Take another swallow.' He supported her head, their sweat mingled. He bunched a blanket to help her keep her head raised, gave her a final swallow of whiskey, then went to work with the shirtsleeve and warm water. She twisted feebly to watch the driver who was roughly cradling her second-born in powerful arms, swaying the baby from side to side and ignoring its ear-splitting wails. The driver saw her watching, grinned all across his face, and winked at her.

'This one'll be riding a rough string before you know it, ma'am. My last one looked just like this, and now's he's pushing nine, big as his brothers and strong as oak.' The driver paused to consider the squirming baby. 'I'd call him Abe, ma'am. For President Lincoln. He's got dark hair, and he's sort of wrinkled and ugly like President Lincoln.'

Frank sat back, drying his hands and looking at Ella Leland, his expression rueful. 'There never was a tactful coach-driver, ma'am. I think he's a very handsome boy. In fact I think both your boys are very handsome.'

She smiled feebly. 'May I hold him, now?'

They gave her the baby, then hovered because he was strong and fretful, and she was weak, but she did not drop him.

Frank picked up the bottle, handed it to the driver, then arose to spring the kinks out of his cramped legs before walking to the trough for a long drink of cold water, and a two-handed rinsing. Finally, he sank down upon the edge of the smooth old stones and watched the woman and her child, spring-water and salt-sweat mingling down the front of him.

The gunguard returned, with John, their eyes fixed upon the prostrate woman with the gasping, complaining baby over beneath the immense old bull-pines. They stopped near Frank at the trough, with the gunguard saying, 'No trouble? I seen an In'ian woman one time, had lots of trouble.' He wagged his head. 'They ought to have a regulation on the line—no female passengers if they're very far along.'

Frank ignored the guard and looked at John Leland. 'You've got a brother.'

John did not take his eyes off his mother. 'I know, because I heard him crying.'

Frank considered that. A sister would also have cried. Evidently, in the Leland family, they had not thought about a girl. Well; neither had the driver, so maybe this was how it was supposed to work out.

The driver walked back to the trough and handed back Frank's whiskey bottle. Then he said, 'Mister Kandelin, I got to get on down to town. If you want, I'll send someone back with a wagon full of straw, and the doctor.'

Frank was agreeable. 'Ask the town marshal to hunt up my rangeboss; he'll be at the depot expecting me. Have my rangeboss get a rig from the liverybarn and come up here.' Frank handed back the bottle. 'Keep it.'

The driver and gunguard went over to their coach and climbed up. They leaned to wave to the woman. She waved back, weakly, then the big vehicle turned clear and got back onto the roadway, heading down-country with the rear-wheel brakes rubbing to help hold the rig back.

Frank looked at John. 'What do you think, pardner?'

The lad's answer was predictable. 'Will my mother be all right?' and when Frank assured John his mother would be just fine, John then said, 'Mister Kandelin, do you have any of those sardines left; I'm hungry.'

Chapter Three

THE FK TRAIL

Curtis Hyatt had been Kandelin's rangeboss for six years, ever since Kandelin had become big enough to need extra riders and someone to supervise them. In size and build, even in coloring, Curtis and Frank Kandelin were alike. In outlook, they did not differ very much, either, but when the stage-driver found Curtis at the depot, instead of seeking Bert Holton the town constable as Kandelin had instructed the driver to do, and personally explained to the rangeboss where his employer was, and what Frank had done up there, with that pregnant woman, Curtis's mouth dropped open and he regarded the driver with disbelief. Then he said, 'I knew it'd be something. I knew, the minute they told me inside, that the coach was 'way past due, Frank had got himself into something.'

The driver offered a mildly defensive rebuttal. 'It

wasn't *him*, it was the lady had the baby.'

Curtis did not argue, he went down to the livery-barn, hired a rig, had them fill the back with clean straw, borrowed two clean horse-blankets, and drove out, heading for the divide, with a hostler standing back there scratching his head.

It was not a long drive and the day would remain sunbright and pleasant for hours yet, so Curtis did not hurry, which was just as well since Ella Leland needed time for recovery.

She rallied slowly, but well; she was strong, and as healthy as an ox, and when Frank good-naturedly told her of Indian women going behind a bush to have their babies, then drying them off as they joined the march, Ella smiled and said, 'If I had to do that, I suppose I could. But I don't have to, do I?'

He squatted beside her. The baby was snuffling in his sleep, making small, jerky movements. John had gone to the center of the road to watch for a rig coming upland from Bivouac.

Frank offered Ella a tomato tin of cold water, which she accepted and drained to the very bottom. As he was rising to get her a refill, she said, 'Without you, Mister Kandelin, I don't know what I would have done.'

He answered quietly. 'You'd have managed.'

Her eyes twinkled ironically at him. 'Yes, I know. Like the Indian woman.'

He brought back more water. She was very thirsty. He also washed her face with the cool, damp cloth, and after an hour he dug in his valise for a clean pair of underdrawers, and left them with her while he sauntered out where John was keeping his vigil. The boy raised an arm.

'There's a light wagon coming, Mister Kandelin.'

Frank looked and nodded. That would be Curtis, and he would have something sarcastic to say, but he wouldn't say it as long as the woman was with them, he would simply *look* it.

'Mister Hyatt,' Frank told John. 'FK rangeboss.'

John kept studying the small, far-distant oncoming wagon. 'FK—is that you—Frank Kandelin?'

'Yep.'

John turned. 'Is this all your land, up here?'

'Yep. Seven thousand acres of it, John.' Frank pointed. 'The buildings are yonder, northwest of town up through those clearings and beyond the trees.'

The boy's dark eyes never wavered. 'Can my mother and I go home with you, until she's better, Mister Kandelin?'

He dropped his arm and squinted down where the rig was stirring thin dust, stopped dead in his tracks by the boy's question. For a fact, it would be a few days before the woman would be up to traveling by stage again, and in Bivouac, although there was a rooming-house, it wasn't what the woman needed. He did not know what to say. The idea had not occurred to him before, and now when it did, it caused considerable discomfort. On the other hand, Frank Kandelin was a man of sound judgments and reasonable decisions. He

26

was the only friend the woman had, in the Bivouac countryside—and it would be for only a few days.

He nodded towards the boy. 'I think that's a good idea,' he said, and was rewarded for this decision by the look on the boy's face. He laid a hand lightly upon John's shoulder. 'Stay here, and when Mister Hyatt arrives, tell him to back the rig over by the trough so we can hoist your mother into it.'

Ella's eyes were closed, her breathing was deep and even, as though she were sleeping, so when Frank paused and looked down, believing she was drowsing, and she opened her eyes looking straight up at him, he said, 'You can sleep for about another hour, if you'd like, before the rig gets up here. It's coming; John spotted it from the roadway.'

She had the baby cuddled close. It was limp and snuffling in its sleep, as wrinkled as a prune and appealingly helpless.

He knelt. 'John and I decided you'll come to my place and rest up until you're fit to go on up to Moab.'

The blue eyes clung to his face. 'We can't do that, Mister Kandelin.'

He smiled a little. 'Yeah, I know you can't, Mrs. Leland, but you will.' He picked up the cloth and wiped her face gently. Then he leaned for a closer look at the baby.

Her eyes never left him. When he rocked back and saw her expression, he sighed. 'Don't be stubborn. Anyway, you owe me a favor. So you'll spend a few days at the ranch. It won't be too bad. We've got water

27

piped into the mainhouse, and plenty of bedrooms. You'll have all the privacy you need. I have three riders and a rangeboss. No women, but we'll fetch one out from town if you need help.'

Her mouth quivered and she turned quickly towards the child in her arms. Frank arose and walked slowly over to the trough for a drink of water, then he cocked his head, listening to the grinding cadence of shod hooves and steel wagon-wheels coming up the last grade to the summit.

When Curtis Hyatt saw the boy in the center of the road, and waved, John waved back. Then Curtis saw Frank, and drove on up without waving, just eyeing Frank with a caustic look. Frank gestured for the rig to be swung about and backed in. This was accomplished without a word being passed between them. When Curtis set the brake, looped the lines and climbed down, holstered Colt striking the wooden brake-handle, Frank pointed to Ella Leland, speaking for the first time. 'We'll fix her comfortably in the back, then head for home. One of the men can take the wagon back in the morning.'

Curtis tugged at his gloves, eyeing the woman with the baby. Then he turned and saw the dark-eyed boy looking straight up at him, and finally he faced Frank.

Kandelin held up a hand. 'Later,' he said. 'Now lend me a hand getting her into the rig.' Frank lowered the tailgate. 'John; climb up there and kind of scuff that straw around, then spread the blankets atop it.' He turned, avoiding the look of his rangeboss. 'Let's go.'

Ella was not very heavy. She might have been, if there had only been one man to lift her into the wagon-bed, but Curtis Hyatt was a powerfully-built, very strong individual, and so was Frank Kandelin. They made her comfortable, with the baby in her arms and John in the straw beside her, then Frank introduced his rangeboss, and Curtis gravely lifted his hat.

She smiled at him. 'I'll never be able to repay all this kindness, Mister Hyatt. There are wonderful people out here.'

Curtis acknowledged this impassively. 'Yes'm. And Mister Kandelin's right handy at things like this.'

Frank left them, walked to the front and climbed to the rough board seat. When Curtis secured the tailgate and also climbed up to head out, Frank said, 'I brought back a quart of whiskey from Tucson, but we had to use it . . . You don't need it anyway.'

The route to FK's headquarters-ranch was down the stageroad almost to Bivouac, then northwesterly up through a dense stand of thorny old chaparral, out across two bare, grassy top-outs, and down across a sparsely timbered big meadow and around the base of a flat-topped hill into a long trough of land, perhaps two miles long but only about a mile wide. There was a running spring in the center of this swale, and there were crumbling remains of ancient Indian camps all up through this place. There was also a ghostly old four-walled adobe structure whose roof had fallen in years earlier, to indicate someone beside tribesmen had utilized this spring-fed long meadow, but the adobe ruin was a mile north of where Frank Kandelin's log buildings stood. No one, in the days when that adobe house had been erected, would build a house anywhere near trees. Where Frank had put up his log barn, bunkhouse, wagon and shoeing sheds, and his low, long mainhouse, there were cottonwoods and white oaks. It was a wonderfully shady place in summertime. No one had worried about trees hiding skulking redskins for almost a full decade, by the time Frank had settled on this place for his home-ranch.

He'd had a cow camp here for three years prior to starting the buildings, and when the light buggy finally made it around the knoll and up the trough, it passed through what had once been a rather extensive Indian village, but about all that was still visible were the stone rings, a few graves upon a sidehill, notable for the rock cairns marking them, and some sunken, circular places where hide hogans had stood. It was dusk, though, so the people in the wagon scarcely noticed any of this.

They were instead more intent upon the pale lamplight ahead at the log bunkhouse.

One cowboy was at the barn when Curtis tooled the rig up out front. He stood like a statue, staring at the young boy in the back, and the woman with the baby in her arms. Then he turned without speaking and gravely marched to the lighted bunkhouse, to disappear inside.

Frank took Ella and her two sons up to the main-

30

house. Curtis was still at the barn piling harness from the livery horse when three solemn rangeriders walked over to the doorway of the barn and stood there, lined up and staring.

Curtis said, 'Well; couple of you park the damned wagon, and close your mouths before a bat flies in.' He led the livery horse to a corral and freed it, then closed the gate and turned. The three cowboys were still standing there.

'The lady had a baby at the divide,' he stated, irritably. 'She and Frank was on the same stage. Frank pulled the baby, and now she's going to stay with us for a few days, until she's fit to travel. She's got a husband up at Moab—or somewhere, anyway. And what's so unusual about women having babies?'

A bow-legged, squatty, frog-built cowboy, grey and scarred, answered quietly. 'Nothin'. Except Frank never brought one home before.' He turned. 'Let's park the damned wagon.'

Curtis went over to lend his weight. They got the rig pushed clear of the barn opening, then the same frog-like cowboy, whose name was Simon Bowers, leaned, gazing up at the lighted mainhouse. 'They don't bring good luck with 'em,' he mused aloud. 'Once, I worked at a cow camp down in—.'

'Oh for Chriz' sake,' groaned Curtis Hyatt. 'She couldn't help it. The baby just *came*, that's all.'

A thin, wide-shouldered younger cowboy, named Slim Morrow, had a certain contribution to offer. 'What's wrong with a woman bein' on the place,

31

Simon? I'll tell you what—her cooking's bound to be better'n our'n.'

Curtis scowled. 'She won't be here that long. Just a few days. Until she gets her legs under her. Then she goes up to Moab to find her damned husband . . . And what kind of a man brings a woman in *that* shape, all the way out from the east, anyway?'

'Where, in the east?' asked the swarthy cowboy, whose slightly hawkish cast of features hinted at Indian blood.

'Ohio,' stated Curtis. 'Frank told me on the drive.'

The hawk-faced rider, called Tomahawk by his friends who knew no other name for him, and who never offered any other name, pursed his lips and put his jet-black gaze upon the mainhouse. 'Ohio. That's where Custer come from. Ohio.'

The thin, younger rider turned. 'You mean *General* Custer?'

'Yeah. He come from Ohio,' said Tomahawk, then he shrugged. 'But she's a woman.'

Curtis rolled up his eyes to the faint starlight. 'I never figured you'd notice she was a woman,' he exclaimed. 'Now—can we go over to the cookshack? I'm hungry enough to gnaw the back end out of a skunk if someone'd hold its head.'

The night arrived softly, as it usually did this late in springtime, softly and gently, and with a canopy of cobalt-blue punctuated by diamond-chip bright tiny stars.

A wolf howled, but the men at the cookshack did

not hear it. The boy with his nose pushed flat against the window-glass of his mother's bedroom, heard it though, and held his breath for a moment. Then he turned solemnly and stared at his mother's back, where she was sitting upon the edge of the bed feeding her second-born. She did not appear to have heard the wolf, either. Right then, she probably would not have heard a salvo of cannon fire.

Chapter Four

A WORLD OF MEN

Tomahawk was obdurate. 'Cradle hell,' he told the others, out by the corrals. 'You cut willow-reeds while they're green, and you shape them like this, you see— to form a basket. Then, when they dry, they're hard, and you shove moss down at the lower end of this thing, and you lines the inside with red cloth, and then you tie the baby in it and—.'

'What's the moss for?' asked Curtis.

Tomahawk looked disgustedly at the rangeboss. 'They wet, don't they?' he demanded. 'And that ain't all they do in a cradle-board. Well, when the moss is wet, you reach in from below, pull the stuff out, then shove more moss back up there.'

The men were impressed, but when Frank walked

up, Simon seemed to be having second thoughts, because he said, 'Frank; it ain't an In'ian baby, is it?'

Kandelin stopped in his tracks. 'A what?'

'Well; Tomahawk's been telling us how to make a squaw-pack for the little kid, and it seems to me that if it ain't an In'ian kid, it won't do well in something like that.'

Frank looked at Tomahawk, then at them all, and finally he said, 'She's got it bedded down in a dresser-drawer. She pulled the drawer out and—.'

'It'll fall out,' exclaimed Slim, shifting his position against the front of the pole corral. 'When they're that little they can get busted pretty easy.'

Simon beamed. 'I got the solution. We can take one of the horseshoe kegs, cut it in half, bind it with some steel strap, set some legs under it, and line it with blankets.' He looked around. 'What's wrong with that?'

No one answered. It took a little time to grasp the idea; in fact it had taken them half the morning just to grasp the idea that they had an infant and a woman on the ranch.

Curtis suddenly said, 'Hell; what'll we do if it gets sick? We're seven miles from town, and you can't get old Doc Severns out here unless someone's dying.'

Simon would not be distracted, and the more he dwelt upon his idea for a cradle, the better he liked it. 'First things first,' he told Curtis, sternly. 'Frank, you got anything special needs doing this morning? If not I'd like to get right to work on the cradle.'

Frank turned to eye the horses beyond, in the corral. There was always riding to be done this time of the year, but it wasn't *critical* riding. They were pretty well-calved out, and the cattle were to their knees in feed. He could have said Mrs. Leland didn't need a cradle, that she wouldn't be on the ranch long enough to use a cradle, and when she took the stage north to Moab from Bivouac, she couldn't very well haul a horseshoe-keg cradle along with her, but all he *did* say was, 'No. Go ahead, Simon. Curt, you can go north with Tomahawk and Slim and lay down some scent where someone said they saw those two cougars last week.' He turned towards the barn to get a bridle before heading back to catch one of the corralled horses.

John Leland was standing over near the front of the mainhouse, dark eyes fixed upon Frank. A man would have had to have been made of stone not to have been able to pick up the emanations. Frank slackened pace, then turned towards his riders and said, 'Curt, you fellers rig out something for John and take him with you.'

The cowboys gazed past Frank, who went along to the barn, eyeing the stripling youth. They were rough men. Not unkind, but hard and rough and unrelenting in their demands upon others to be just as honest at their jobs and just as rough and selfless in doing their work. They knew nothing at all about young boys, except what instinct and two-thirds forgotten memory told them.

Tomahawk looked at the corralled horses. 'There's Blaze,' he said to Curtis. 'Dog-gentle—unless he steps on a snake.'

Curtis acquiesced. 'Rig him out, Tomahawk.' Then Curtis started ahead towards the motionless, very erect youngster.

Frank got a horse and led it to the barn to be saddled. He heard the boy's piping voice and watched as Curtis, tall and strong, passed the front of the barn heading for the corral, for all the world like a five-year-old bull being tagged after by a yearling bull. Frank smiled to himself.

The boy would learn something today about several things, and riding horses would only be a small part of it. He would also learn something about rangemen, about the varied things they did, instead of chasing bandits or turning back stampedes, the things penny magazines inferred was their daily commitment.

When Frank rode out of the yard heading for Bivouac, he saw Tomahawk hand the boy a bridle and point to the old blue-roan called Blaze. The boy stood looking helpless, and all Tomahawk did was tell him to catch the horse.

It would be a bruising day for the boy.

The ride to town could be made in good time providing the day was cool and the horse under a man was sound and willing. This particular day, though, Frank was in no hurry. He only had two reasons for making the ride, and one of them—trying to get old

Doctor Severns to drive out and look at Ella Leland and the infant—did not appear to be anything requiring haste. The other thing, to take his wallet-full of money to the bank for deposit, was nothing that would require haste either.

He had sold the biggest gather he'd ever trailed out, last autumn, and had been over to Tucson last week to get the last of his payment for them. As he loped overland he tried to project his production for the next two years, and if the weather would favor him, predators could be kept away, disease and thieves did not hurt him too badly, and the market in Chicago and Kansas City held, that would be all the time he would need to have everything free and clear, and to also have a substantial financial cushion in the Bivouac bank.

The years of exhaustion, grinding hard labor and total dedication were finally beginning to yield their reward. He smiled to himself. The penny magazines never mentioned this side of the range-cattle business either. Probably because the people who wrote for those magazines had no idea under the sun what was required to be a range cattleman.

By the time he had Bivouac in sight, the sun was high, the morning was warm and softly fragrant, and the azure heavens stretched endlessly, and flawlessly.

He rode in from the west, angled towards the liverybarn, and as he was handing over his reins to the hostler, a gruff-voiced, white-bearded, thin and stooped older man with a vinegary expression across a ruddy, lined face, called over as he stiffly descended from a dusty top-buggy.

Doctor Severns had been a surgeon during the War Between the States, and although everything else had changed since those distant days, Matthew Severns's attitude and disposition had not. He beat dust from his rusty black coat and stamped over where Frank was, to say, 'Well; I heard all about you delivering the child up at the divide.' Severns raised keen, shrewd blue eyes the color of new ice. 'Where are they?'

'At the ranch, Doc, and that's partly why I rode in today.'

'I don't go out of town and you know it,' snapped the older man.

'Well, she's not in shape to make the ride, Doctor.'

'Why not, confound it; squaws do it, and during the war I saw new mothers fleeing with babes in their arms, astraddle mules.'

Frank let the hostler walk away leading his ranch-horse, before speaking again. 'All right, Doc. I'll wait, then fetch her in. She'd ought to be able to ride in a wagon in a few days, hadn't she?'

'Of course. That's the trouble nowadays,' stated Matthew Severns. 'Coddle females. Everyone treats 'em like they're made of glass. Frank, this country was founded by a different breed of folks. In *those* days womenfolk stood up right beside their men, and when trouble came—.'

'Doc, men wouldn't stand up if they'd just had babies. I thought I was going to be sick to my

38

stomach, up there. That's a hell of a torment to go through.'

Matthew Severns looked up, and for a moment he was silent while he gazed at the younger man. Then he cleared his throat and became gruff again. 'Pshaw! Sick to your stomach! That's the most natural thing under the sun—next to dying, Frank . . . By the way, how old a woman is she?'

Frank pursed his lips. 'Twenty-two or three, maybe.'

'Maybe?'

'How the hell would I know how old she is?'

'You could damned well ask, couldn't you, Frank?'

He *could* have asked, but it had not come up, had not seemed important, and he wouldn't have just come right out and asked *any* woman her age, so he said, 'Doc, in your business something like that's important; folks talk to you about their age. In *my* business, a man just doesn't—.'

'Frank, for heavens' sake, when you need to know something, *ask*!'

'I didn't need to know.' Frank suddenly halted in mid-speech. 'She's got a son named John. He's about twelve or thirteen, Doctor.'

Old Severns' ice-blue eyes showed rough irony. 'Well then, she's a damned sight over twenty-two, wouldn't you say?'

That was reasonable because it had to be. Frank nodded his head. 'Yeah. But she *looks* so darned young.'

Matthew Severns made a surprising statement. 'All right then, all right. Just so's I won't have to listen to your whining, I'll drive out there this afternoon. And it'll cost you a dollar!' As though to uphold his reputation for cantankerousness, the physician turned, glaring, in search of the hostler, and when he saw him distantly caring for Kandelin's animal, he yelled at him.

'Well, confound it, Alex, what does a body have to do, stand around here all day waiting for service?'

The dayman sighed, turned and walked on up to lead Doctor Severn's buggy-horse down into the barn. He did not look at the old man as he walked past him.

After the doctor had departed, stooped, scowling, his stride a cross between a crab-like sidling, and a thrusting stamp, the hostler looked over at Frank and said, 'You know, there's one thing folks got to hand old Doc. You never got to worry about what his mood'll be, because it's always gawd-awful.'

Frank walked up the opposite side of the roadway to the brick bank building, and all the while he was transacting his business up there, he was marvelling that Severns had actually volunteered to drive out to the ranch.

Later, with a crisp depositor's slip in his wallet, complete with the bank-manager's own personal, very elegant Spencerian signature, Frank returned to the roadway and was hailed by a thickly put-together man of average, or perhaps even a shade less than average, height. The man looked to be about Frank's own age, but more weathered, more worn. The badge on his vest was carelessly pinned, and in general, the thick man's appearance was not exactly unkempt, but neither was it especially tidy.

His eyes were small and very blue, and when he smiled they were almost entirely hidden in his rugged, scarred face. He was smiling now, when he came up and said, 'Frank; one of the fellers at the saloon has this cow that's been straining for a couple hours now, and he was wondering, you being experienced and all—.'

Kandelin laughed. 'You damned idiot,' he said, and the town marshal laughed in a booming way as he defended himself.

'Folks are saying around town Doc's going to be mad, you taking over his practice and all. By the way, how much do you charge for roadside deliveries?'

Constable Bert Holton was an amiable man, and like all cowboys and former cowboys, he was also an inveterate tease and prankster. But he was also a violent man capable of awesome anger when the occasion arose. He had been a rangerider nine years, and he'd only been Bivouac's town marshal four years; he knew stockmen better than he knew townsmen, but generally, Bert was liked, and those who did not like him, had reason to respect him. He and Frank Kandelin had been close friends for more years than Bert had been the local constable, therefore Frank's response to being teased over delivering the Leland baby was rough retaliation, as when he said, 'The lady was wondering about a name for her little boy, and I thought of you right away.'

Holton's small eyes peered warily. 'Why?'

'Well; the baby's short and thick and ugly as a mud fence, has little weasel eyes and a great big mouth with a tongue inside it that's hinged in the center and flaps at both ends.'

'There's no way for that little kid to be as pretty as me,' exclaimed Constable Holton, 'and you're lyin' when you say he is. Come along, I need a beer. You can tell me about it.'

They headed for the saloon, exchanging rough insults every step of the way.

Chapter Five

FLOWERS IN A COOKSHACK?

The day was drawing to a close when Frank, standing out front of the saloon with Bert Holton, saw Doctor Severns drive by, a fresh horse between the shafts, but otherwise the buggy looked just as dusty, and Doc looked just as vinegary.

Bert strolled to the liverybarn with Frank, still discussing a coach robbery which had occurred southeast of Bivouac the previous week, not because there was any local relevancy, but because Bert thought in terms of things like that, and once he'd mentioned the weather, the price of beef in Chicago or Kansas City, and the condition of the springtime range, about the only fields available to him for open discussion had to do with some facet of crime.

Frank was interested. It also happened that Frank Kandelin was a good listener. He allowed Bert to monopolize the conversation even after they were out front of the barn, after the hostler had been sent to rig out the ranch-horse and fetch him up front. The only time Frank spoke was when Bert finally phrased a statement as though it were a question, and said, 'There's just too damned much of it around nowadays, Frank, and I'm not sure even the cow camps and out-lying ranches won't be hit, are you?'

Kandelin smiled. 'Somebody's in for a hell of a surprise if they raid my place, Bert. I don't think most of the cow outfits would produce much anyway— even if a band of men wouldn't get all shot to hell trying to raid them. No one keeps much money lying around.' He grinned. 'In the cow business, Bert, no one *makes* much money.'

Holton looked pained, but he let that pass because the saddled animal arrived, and Frank took the reins with one hand, passed coins to the hostler with the other hand, then wheeled the horse to mount up as he also said, 'I got to wondering about something up at the saloon, Bert: Do you know anyone up at Moab?'

Bert did. 'Sure; lots of fellers. I also know the

Mormon constable up there. Big, whiskered feller. Why?'

'I'd appreciate it if you'd send a message up there by the daily coach, for someone—the constable, maybe—to hunt down a man named Mike Leland and tell him where his son and wife are—out at my place—and that they'll be along within a few days... The man's probably worrying that his wife didn't show up last night on the coach.'

Constable Holton was agreeable. 'Sure. Be glad to,' and as Kandelin turned away with a nod, Constable Holton lifted his left hand in a casual little salute.

There was plenty of daylight left, even though the day was two-thirds concluded, and Frank felt the same total lack of compulsion for haste returning, as he had felt this morning heading outward.

He had things on his mind. In fact, he usually had a number of things on his mind. It was impossible to be in his business and not be occupied every waking hour, but once a range cowman's gather had been completed, the tally made in springtime, the marking done, the cattle turned out and driven to their first pasture of the new season, most of what else had to be done lay in the hands of Mother Nature. If she would furnish the growing grass, sunlight, and clean creek-water, the cattle would do the rest, and this left the riders at least nominally free to do chores which impinged upon the later work.

They rode—patrolled, actually—and made certain

bulls didn't spend *all* their time in mudholes, drowsing in shady places, or fighting one another. They kept close watch on first-call heifers, and when it was required—although no cowboy liked doing it— when a calf was 'hung-up' they'd profanely dismount and lend a hand. The riding chores were vastly varied and sometimes very demanding, but the kind of work to be done after the turn-out, usually was related more to the maintenance of water holes, salt-logs, predator control, and the everlasting jobs which had to be done around the corrals, buildings, and vehicles. A man might spend three days of the week on horseback, and the other three days on foot with axle-grease to his elbows overhauling wagons, but none of it was actually terribly critical, and it was with this calm assurance that the essential things had been taken care of that Frank rode slowly back to the ranch.

He even had time to consider Ella and her sons, and from this kind of thinking, he went on to another related topic; something he had occasionally thought of over the years without ever doing anything more than thinking about it: A family of his own.

The trouble with any kind of work that required much physical labor, at least among rangemen, was that at days' end they were tired enough to sit and drink some beer, or a couple of slugs of rye whiskey, and reflect upon what they had done and what they still had to do, to the exclusion of softer, more tender thoughts, and when they dropped into bed, they slept like logs.

45

But Frank had occasionally felt an urge, now that he had his buildings, his deeded land, his herds and his sense of success and security, to speculate about this other matter.

In fact, by the time he had the lights in sight through the soft-settling dusk, he was subjectively thinking of Ella and her two boys. He hadn't ever really, seriously, imagined the kind of woman he'd some day marry and raise a family with, but when he remembered her courage, up there at the divide, recalled her smile even when she'd been in pain, and how she'd reacted to him and his efforts to help, it all fit into his idea of what he liked in people; in this instance, it fit into what he admired in anyone, but in a woman particularly.

She did not whine, nor complain, nor resent the situation her husband had got her into, even though she surely must have felt terribly alone, friendless and abandoned, up there under the pines at the top of the pass, giving birth to her child among total strangers.

The more he thought back, the more he admired Ella Leland. By the time he reached the tie-rack out front of the barn, and saw Matthew Severn's dusty old topbuggy over in front of the lighted mainhouse, the more he felt envious towards a man named Mike Leland, whom he had never even seen.

Curtis strolled forth from the bunkhouse and saw Frank dismounting. Curt had slicked down his hair and scrubbed up for supper. He had a brown-paper cigarette dangling unlit from his mouth as he strolled

46

over to take the unsaddled horse to a corral and turn him in. When he strolled back he said, 'Old Brimstone's been up there at the mainhouse with Miz' Leland for a solid hour. She isn't ailing, is she?'

Frank did not think so. She had seemed perfectly normal to him this morning when he'd left the house. He guessed Doctor Severn's visit was being prolonged for other reasons, and said so.

'How often would that flinty old cuss get to visit with a pretty woman, Curt?'

The rangeboss paused to light his cigarette, before accepting this suggestion, then he said, 'How often would any of us get to do that, Frank?' He pointed to the porch out front of the bunkhouse. 'Simon's finished the crib, and you know, I hated to tell him so, but he did a right fine job with it.' Curtis softly smiled. 'He's out back washing up before he hauls it up and presents it to her.' Curtis inhaled and exhaled. 'I reckon because it's springtime, even old mossbacks like Simon get soft in the head.'

Frank could have agreed aloud with that, but he did not get the opportunity. Doc Severns came forth from the front door up across the yard, and both the stalwart cowmen down in darkness by the barn saw the handsome woman framed in lamplight up there, smiling and softly thanking Severns for driving out. She did not look, at that distance anyway, like someone who had recently been through an ordeal.

Then she closed the door and Doc went down to his rig, climbed in, turned the patient horse and started slowly across the yard on his way back to town. Frank stepped over into sight, and Doc hauled back on his lines, then leaned and looked out.

'You owe me a dollar,' he stated.

Frank fished in a pocket then held forth the silver cartwheel. Doc stared at it, then cleared his throat and leaned back, making no move to take the coin.

'Forget it,' he muttered. 'It wasn't *her* fault, and it sure wasn't *your* fault. But if I ever meet up with her husband . . .' Doc removed his hat, placed it upon the seat at his side and regarded Frank candidly. 'He's a lucky man, my boy. That woman's the first female I've seen since I came out here, who put me in mind of my wife.'

Frank had never before heard that Matthew Severns had been married.

'She's got the two main ingredients womenfolk don't seem to have much, any more, Frank. Looks and gumption. Pretty as a picture, and behind that nice smile and those handsome, blue eyes, she's got enough iron up her back to cast a cannon out of. He's a very lucky man. Well, sitting out here isn't going to get me any supper, is it?'

'Eat with us,' said Frank. 'We'd be proud to have you stay and—.'

'The hell I will,' exclaimed the older man. 'I've eaten at man-run cow ranches before. The marvel to me is that the human digestive tract—all the human insides, for that matter—survive the abuse you people heap upon yourselves.' Doctor Severns picked up his

48

lines, nodded, clucked, and drove on out of the yard.

Curtis was smiling from over by the tie-rack, where he'd heard every word.

A squat, unprepossessing dark shadow moved from the side of the bunkhouse to the porch, bristly hair slicked down and shiny. Simon Bowers hoisted the horseshoe-keg cradle in his arms and went directly towards the mainhouse.

Frank watched a moment, then said, 'Hell; this place is getting like Main Street in Tucson, for the traffic. Let's get something to eat.'

The cookshack was an extension of the mainhouse-kitchen. In fact, the mainhouse kitchen cupboards, stove, and utensil racks, were in place along the east wall, separating the mainhouse-parlor from the cook-shack, so actually the cookshack was an integral part of the mainhouse, although it was never referred to in this fashion. It was called by its correct name, as though to imply it was something separate.

Big cow outfits had men who did little but cook. Often, they were old cowboys, and rarely ever were they women, but on ranches with fewer than six or eight hired hands, the cooking was usually parcelled out on an alternating basis. The only exceptions were the men who simply could not cook at all, and when men like Frank Kandelin hired riders, they usually asked if the man could cook a little, and normally the answer was 'yes' even though this variety of cooking, cowboys successfully undertook, was just about as bad as Doc Severns had implied it was.

When Curtis and Frank entered the cookshack from out back, the room was lighted, an uncommonly wonderful aroma permeated the entire atmosphere, and a huge copper kettle was simmering upon the big cooking-range over against the far wall.

Someone had scrubbed the oilcloth atop the long dining table, the plates, cups and utensils had been placed around for five diners, and what stopped Curtis in his tracks was the chili-bowl in the center of the table which had water in it, and which had violet and yellow wildflowers floating in the water.

Frank went to the stove, lifted the pot and sniffed, then gently replaced the lid and turned. 'Curt . . . ?'

The rangeboss made a little helpless gesture. 'Damned if I knew anything about it, Frank. It had to be *her*. Look; flowers on the table. What the hell's in the kettle? I never smelt anything that good in my life.'

Frank slowly examined the room. There was a big bowl of salad, thick slices of fresh sourdough bread, and a fresh pot of coffee simmering. He removed his hat, considered the flowers, then said, 'Curt; hell, she's not in shape for something like this. This is a hell of a lot of work for *anyone* to go to, let alone a woman who's just had a little kid.'

'Well; she must have wanted to do it, Frank, or she sure wouldn't have.'

'Yeah, but Curt, it's not fair. She don't have to feel like she owes us anything . . . I never saw flowers in here before.'

'I never saw flowers inside *any* of the buildings before,' exclaimed the rangeboss. 'You know; now that I think back, maybe I should have suspected something. When the boy came back with Tomahawk and Slim this afternoon, they made him look after his horse, then he disappeared . . . She must have called him up to lend her a hand, because he never came back to the yard.'

Frank got a plate and went over to the kettle. 'I'll talk to her, after I've eaten,' he said. 'You might as well eat too.'

They both ate—and ate.

Chapter Six

A MAN, A WOMAN, AND MOONLIGHT

A woman of Ella Leland's coloring, fair and golden by sunlight, showed tiredness with unavoidable dark shadows around the eyes, and when she smiled at Frank, as pleased at what she had accomplished as a small girl would have been, he noticed the dark shadows, and it bothered his conscience, so he said, 'No one ever did anything that nice around here before,' and he could not make himself scold her, because he knew exactly what her reaction would be—hurt—and she certainly did not deserve to feel

51

that way. 'You must be the best cook ever to come out of Ohio,' he told her, and saw John in the parlor shadows, beaming at this praise of his mother, dark eyes aglow.

'The men are in there eating right now, Miz' Leland. I'm going to have nothing but trouble with them after you folks leave. What kind of stew was that? Tomahawk said you must have learned to cook like that from an Indian woman.'

She laughed, where she was sitting in the big dark leather chair beside the marble-topped lamp-table. 'Not that I know of, Mister Kandelin; my grandmother came from Kentucky, and she taught me to cook when I wasn't much older than John. But I never heard her mention being part Indian.'

She pointed, blue eyes made darker by the shadows under them. 'Simon made that cradle. Isn't he talented, Mister Kandelin? I felt like crying, but I didn't. I think he would have been embarrassed.' She swung slowly to face him again. 'I've never been treated like this before. Well; not since I was a child. Back in Ohio they said Westerners were savages and lived like the Indians, and went around shooting people . . .' She clasped her hands and watched his bronzed face a moment. 'You are wonderful people.'

Frank looked over and saw John looking steadily at him. He beckoned. 'Don't hang back, boy, come right on up. How's your rump?'

John's eyes jumped wide open. His mother's jaw sagged. Frank saw his error, and with color coming

52

upwards into his face, he tried hard to mitigate his bluntness. 'Well; usually when folks haven't ridden a lot, and they get put through the hoops, they are sore.' He looked for help at Ella. 'It's just the way men talk. It doesn't mean anything.'

She looked at her son. 'Are you sore, John?'

The boy stoutly shook his head. 'No. But we covered a heap of ground.'

Ella's arched brows leveled out slightly. 'A heap—John?'

'Yes'm. That's how cowboys say it—we covered a heap of ground.'

Ella subsided, softly. 'Oh.'

Frank Kandelin, looking from one of them to the other, came to a decision. 'Miz' Leland, he's right, and I expect that up around Moab you'll have another problem to cope with; miners talk pretty rough. Rougher than cattlemen.' He smiled at her. 'Just so's you'll know what to watch for.'

She returned Frank's gaze soberly, without speaking until he arose to depart, and said, 'I asked the constable at Bivouac to get in touch with the constable at Moab, so's your husband won't be worrying about you not arriving.'

Her response was a little unsteady. 'Mister Kandelin—about Moab: What is it like, up there?'

He would have liked to have been able to lie to her with a clear conscience, but he couldn't, so he answered truthfully. 'It's a mining town, Miz' Leland. The buildings are new, mostly made of green wood, the road's a swamp all winter long, and there are six saloons along the front roadway. There was talk up there, last year, about building a school. It's—a frontier town. Maybe Mister Leland's built a cabin up one of the draws, which would be best because then you'd have a garden patch, and some privacy.' Frank's candid opinion of Moab was that of all the rough towns he'd been in, Moab had the least to be said in its favor. He did not tell her this, though. He did not make it better than it was, except to hold out a little hope that it might improve.

'I'd guess that within the next five or ten years, Moab'll settle down, Miz' Leland,' He smiled at her. 'All these towns had to be pioneered.'

From a back room the baby wailed, and Ella was on her feet instantly, heading for that fretful crying. Frank watched her leave, then turned and saw the solemn expression upon the boy's face, and because it was easier to talk to the boy, even though he *was* just a child, Frank said, 'Wish you folks were staying on in Bivouac.'

John's dark eyes never left Kandelin's face. 'Wish we could stay right here,' he replied. Before Frank recovered from that, the boy was speaking again. 'Do you know where General Custer came from, Mister Kandelin?'

Frank looked gravely downward. 'Ohio, wasn't it?'

'No sir. He came from Michigan. Tomahawk said Ohio, but that's wrong.'

Frank considered. 'Are you sure, son?'

'Yes sir. I read it in the newspapers back home.'

Tomahawk could not read, of course, but even so, since newspapers were very rare around Bivouac, if he had been able to read, Tomahawk probably would never have discovered his error. 'Did you explain to him he was wrong?' Frank asked, and John shook his head.

'No sir.'

'Why not?'

'I'm not supposed to correct older people.'

Frank ran a hand up the side of his face, then decided not to say anything; if Ella had taught the boy manners like that, it was up to her to do whatever had to be done about it.

'Well anyway,' Frank murmured, 'he got what was coming to him.'

John stared. 'You mean General Custer?'

'Yeah.'

John continued to stare, but he did not open his mouth, and Frank, watching the lad's expression, got a feeling that now *he* was the one the lad would not correct. It annoyed him, for some obscure reason, so he sat down again before speaking.

'John; what happened at the Little Big Horn wouldn't have ended like it did, if the General hadn't abandoned his field-guns and rushed down in there like a—darned—fool.'

The lad's dark eyes never wavered. Nor did he offer a single comment, and this made Frank feel as though he were taking unfair advantage of the boy, so he threw up his hands, and changed the topic. 'How did you like riding out, today?'

Instead of directly replying, the boy let loose a rush of tumbling words. 'I'm going to be a cowboy when I'm big enough. I never wanted to be a miner anyway. I'll come back someday, and work on FK. Tomahawk said if I was going to be around, he and Slim would make me into a tophand. They'd teach me to ride broncs and rope at the marking ground and work the irons and tend the fire and—.'

'Whoa!' Frank laughed and leaned back in his chair. 'All right; when you're big enough you come back, and I'll sure try you out. Now, you'd better get to bed, hadn't you?'

'Yes sir, because Simon's going to shoe horses in the morning and he promised to let me watch, so's I can learn about that, too.'

Frank sighed. 'Good night, John.'

As the lad was leaving the room, Frank arose and went over to the front door, stepped out upon his long front porch, and studied the high, soft sky and its infinite galaxies. A boy that age would be a trial; underfoot, awkward, exasperating, an endless trial to a grown man's patience—but as the years passed and he grew straight and strong . . . .

The door opened softly behind him. Ella came out with a shawl round her shoulders, and stood beside him at the porch railing. 'The little one is asleep,' she announced quietly, 'but John's in there wide awake. Mister Kandelin; I don't want him bothering you or

56

the riders. Tomorrow I'll keep him at the house. He can help me around—.'

'You can't do that, Miz' Leland,' Frank said quickly. 'Simon's going to show him how a man shoes horses.'

She turned to face him, her handsome face made ten years younger by soft moonlight. She looked amused. 'Will he ever really have to know how to shoe horses, Mister Kandelin? Anyway, I know he's a bother around the riders.'

Frank denied her statement, and ignored her question. 'He's not a bother. Let me tell you something; when I was his age I lived in a town. My paw had the saddle and harness works. I learned his trade, but I only worked there so's I'd be around when the rangemen came in. I wanted to be a cowman from the time I was big enough to straddle a sewing-horse. My paw wanted me in the harness business.'

'And . . . ?'

He gestured with one arm. 'Here I am. I hauled water, cut wood for branding fires, got cuffed by men, kicked by horses and treed by old cows with horns four feet long.' He smiled down into her lifted face. 'Whatever a boy really wants to do—short of robbing banks, ma'am—let him do it, because if you don't, he's going to do it anyway, but he's going to have to waste a lot of years, first.'

She kept looking up at him, but before she spoke she turned to gaze out across the starlit big empty ranch yard. The lamp glowed from two tiny

57

bunkhouse windows, otherwise night was in solid control.

'My husband,' she said quietly, 'was a gunsmith back in Ohio, but he was always a restless man, Mister Kandelin, and when we heard there was a gold strike out here, he sold out. He left us money and came out here. He was never very good at letter-writing, so about all I heard was that he'd arrived, and was mining. Then he wrote the last time for me to come out to him.'

There was nothing in her *words*, but there was something in her *voice* that made Frank consider her lovely profile with a stirring sense of something— foreboding, misgiving—something anyway, that was unpleasant. He reached for a chair and set it close by for her. She sat down and said, 'Honestly, I was frightened half to death, and when we left Fort Sunday to come across all that terrible emptiness—all that burned out desert country—I had to keep looking far ahead where there were trees, or I'd have given up— which of course I couldn't do, could I?' She looked gently at him. 'You were being generous a little while ago, when you talked about Moab, weren't you?'

He eased down upon the porch railing before speaking. 'I was being *hopeful*, ma'am. Like I said, in the house, it takes pioneering to make frontier towns into something else. If the mines don't play out, which happens pretty often in this country, why then I'd say that within a few years Moab'll tame down and get cleaned up.'

'Play out? I thought gold mines went on and on, Mister Kandelin.'

'Some do, Mrs. Leland, but it seems to me that mostly, they yield for a few years, maybe only a few months, then they play out and everyone ups stakes and heads for the next strike. But I'm only speaking from what I've seen out here; I'm no miner.' Frank paused to consider the uppermost thought in his mind, then he decided to put it into words.

'Some parts of Arizona have big mines that've been producing for years. Over in California they've got mines that've been giving up rich ore for an awful long time, the Mexicans and Spaniards worked them before we took over. But in *Northern* Arizona, ma'am, and southern Utah, I don't know of a single gold mine that's been producing for more than maybe a few years. Maybe there are such mines, but I've never heard of them.'

'And the people move on—like gypsies, Mister Kandelin?'

'Well; if a man's a miner, ma'am, he goes where the mines are being worked.' Frank was uncomfortable. For one thing, being honest with someone could make a man feel a lot less than heroic. For another thing, he had just learned something about Ella Leland. She saw straight to the point of things, she did not harbor any delusions. She knew exactly what he was thinking, and he hadn't wanted her to do that.

He shifted position slightly, and saw her turn to look up. He smiled. 'It's a beautiful night,' he said.

She smiled back, understanding perfectly. 'This is beautiful country, Mister Kandelin. It's almost as wonderful as the people in it.'

She arose to go inside, and after they parted Frank continued to sit on the porch railing for a while, until the light went out down at the bunkhouse, then he arose and yawned, and decided that whoever that was who had said beautiful women were lacking in intelligence, had not known Ella Leland.

Then he too, went indoors to bed down.

Chapter Seven

DEAD MEN!

Simon was already at it, over in the shoeing shed, when Frank left the cookshack with Curtis, discussing the work to be lined out for the next couple of days. They could see John in that shady old sooty building, perched like a buzzard upon an up-ended horseshoe keg, watching every move Simon made.

Frank was pocketing the list of things to be brought back from town when he half-smiled and said, 'You've got to hand the lad one thing, Curt; he sure doesn't lie abed.'

'That's a start,' conceded the rangeboss. 'My uncle used to say the earlier a man rises in the morning, the

60

bigger head-start he gets on everyone else in the world.'

They went to the corral and both snaked out a saddle animal. Slim and Tomahawk were just emerging from the cookshack, and Curtis had something to say about that, too. 'Never liked to see men fed too well on a cow outfit; they get to watchin' the sun so's they can bust out for home early.'

Frank's retort ended this speculation. 'Not today, Curt. I scraped the bottom of the kettle for the last of her stew.'

They went to saddle up, and as the ambling pair of riders crossed the yard, and also saw John in the shed with Simon, they called over, teasing him. John's smile was as broad as his features would allow.

Frank left the yard on a big four-year-old green-broke brown colt, concentrating on his mount to the absolute exclusion of everything else for the first two miles, or until the big colt stopped feeling to Frank like he was a humped-up stick of dynamite, and settled down to a slogging, fast walk.

In fact, the farther Frank got from the ranch the less inclined he was to open the colt up and let him have his run; sometimes they didn't just run; sometimes they bogged their heads and bucked blue-blazes—and Frank did not cherish the idea of having to walk back.

But the big, powerhouse-colt turned out to have a good head on his neck. He didn't even shy even when he had a wonderful opportunity, as a covey of sage hens sprang awkwardly into the air and exploded in all directions. The colt squatted like he *would* shy, but when the last clumsy bird had bumbled along out of sight, the colt eased back out of his crouch and walked ahead.

There were a few soiled, raggedy-edged clouds drifting down from the north. They could presage rainfall, or they could only be tantalizingly visible. Folks in town did not want rain. Folks on the ranges almost always wanted it, especially in summertime. Frank rode along through the increasing fresh good warmth of early morning, trying to guess whether the clouds were 'teasers' or whether there was a genuine battery of blacker, more massive clouds beyond them northward, on the far side of the Abajos.

He gave it up, finally, when the clouds seemed to stop moving. He did not stop gazing off in that direction, though. Moab was up there, a fair distance northward, but still up there. It was a hell of a place to take a woman like Ella Leland, and it was also a hell of a place to try and raise two little boys.

What kind of a man would Mike Leland be, not to realize that a woman like his wife, shouldn't be subjected to the kind of an existence awaiting her in Moab, and the kind of looks and perhaps even whispered remarks, she would be subjected to, on that woman-starved territory?

By the time he had rooftops in sight down across the last grassy vale and out through the thin fringe of pines where Bivouac stood, he was ready to dislike a man he had never seen, and had not even heard very much about.

But Bivouac stopped all that, when he was close enough to see the dust in the roadway, down there, and what seemed like a great deal of confusion. Curiosity encouraged him to boot out the big brown colt. He swung southward, as he always did, and came down into town from the open country beyond the corrals of the liverybarn. As he stepped to earth and led his horse up inside, a man standing midway up the wide, shadowy runway whirled and stared.

Frank nodded at the man. 'What's going on?' he asked.

The hostler was erect and tense. 'They robbed the bank,' he exclaimed. 'They blew out one wall. That was the first I knew there was anything wrong at all. This gawddamned explosion liked to stunned me and scairt the whey out of every horse in here. Then I heard the gunfire and run up and looked out.'

Frank's surprise came and went in a flash. He shoved the brown colt's reins at the man and broke ahead in a rush towards the roadway.

There were two men lying flat out up the roadway, one over in front of the log jailhouse, the second man, larger and shaggy-headed, face down over in front of the bank.

No one was near either man, but there were people here and there, timidly coming forth from stores up and down the roadway. The dust was still in the air. Frank could distinctly discern the smell of burnt powder as he ran towards the man out front of the jail-house.

Finally, a small band of men armed with rifles and shotguns appeared, but they did not even glance at the men in the sunlighted roadway, they rushed in the direction of the bank, up where both front glass windows had been blown outward, with some of the glass shards reaching completely to the opposite side of the wide roadway.

Frank dropped to one knee beside the man out front of the jailhouse, picked away the hat and gently eased the man over. It was Bert Holton. He had a bluish, puckery hole under his left eye. He stared sightlessly straight up at Frank.

Doctor Severns, in shirtsleeves, came scuttling along, small black bag in one taloned-fist. Frank eased back as Severns stopped and looked. The medical man did not have to kneel and make an examination. He had seen them like that by the hundreds, back during the war.

'Dead,' he pronounced. 'Put the hat back over his face, Frank. No sense in children and womenfolk having to look at that.'

Doc stepped around and went stalking up in the direction of the man lying face-down in front of the bank. Behind this man, a saddled horse with a pair of worn old cavalry saddlebags and a dirty grey leather tarp rolled professionally around a bedroll, stood uneasily in the wake of all that had happened around him. He belonged to the man in the sunbright dust.

64

Frank picked Bert up and carried him inside the jailhouse, laid him out upon a bunk in one of the cages, then went back and leaned in the doorway looking up where Doc was down on both knees, thin, frail old hands busily working. Evidently the other man wasn't dead.

A paunchy man walked over from the direction of the general store and stopped out in sunlight. 'I saw you pack Bert inside,' he said, face twisted. 'Is he hurt bad?'

'Dead,' replied Frank. 'Who's that man up yonder?'

'One of them,' said the storekeeper. 'I saw them run out a minute after they blew the wall out. That feller came last.'

Frank kept watching Doc, bent over, white head and white shirt intensely bright in the morning sunlight. 'I didn't hear a damned thing,' he muttered, more to himself than to the storekeeper. 'No gunshots, no blast. How long ago did it happen?'

'Few minutes,' replied the storekeeper, losing interest now that he'd learned the constable was dead, and edging away as though to go up and stare at the man Doc was working over. 'Only a few minutes ago—maybe fifteen.'

An old man with a drooping big old dragoon moustache, much stained with tobacco-juice, ambled into the shade of the jailhouse overhang and quietly said, 'That dumb bastard.' He was looking up where a small crowd was gathering around Doc and the man in the

65

roadway. '*Any*body knows better'n to more'n loop their reins when they know blasted well they're going to come a-runnin' and yank the horse loose to fling aboard him. That damned idiot had his reins *tied*. Would you believe that? He stood there, with them other fellers already astraddle hooking hell out'n their mounts up the roadway—he stood there trying to pull loose the rein-knot.'

Frank looked out at the old man. He was a gaunt, tall, rawboned old individual, with a face blasted right out of an existence which had never been mild. Frank said, 'Who shot him?'

The old man leaned to expectorate off the plankwalk before replying. 'Who *didn't*, would be more like it, mister. Everyone in the harness shop and over at the abstract office come boiling out when that dynamite blast went off. Hell; they even fired down *this* way, which was plumb in the opposite direction. I never seen so many silly townsmen with guns in their paws before in my whole life.' The old man let fly again, out into the dust. 'If that feller's still alive, by gawd it's the miracle of all time, mister.'

Frank turned back and went to stand in the doorway looking at dead Bert Holton. If there was ever any consolation to this kind of death, it had to arise from the fact that it was instantaneous. He went in, picked up Bert's gun, spun the cylinder, then tossed it back upon the cot. The Colt had not been fired. Bert must have reacted like everyone else, when that bank wall was blown out; he must have charged out of his

66

office—and no doubt one of the bank-robbers, stationed outside for just this occasion, had dropped Bert in his tracks, not fifteen feet from the jailhouse front door.

Now, finally, people were calling loudly back and forth, and the activity out in the roadway became bedlam. No one came to the jailhouse, although Frank went back and opened the door. The reason they didn't become clear the moment Frank saw that paunchy storekeeper over across the road, gesturing with both arms and bellowing at the leaderless men in the roadway, telling them that the outlaws had killed Bert Holton, and for them to get their guns and horses and be quick about it.

Many men turned to obey.

Frank walked out, heading up the roadway. By now, though, there was no way for anyone not already pressing in around Doc, to see the man he was working over. But Frank heard Doc's voice raised in furious indignation.

'You're worse'n a bunch of vultures, confound it! Get back, blast you, and some of you fetch along a heavy blanket or a piece of canvas we can use to stretcher this man over to my office on.'

A reedy-voiced man said, 'Get away from him, Doc, and I'll save you a lot of time, and the rest of us the cost of caring for that son of a bitch. Doc; get away from him!'

Severns's voice rose. He was not, normally, a profane man, but this time he was. 'You asinine simpleton, you, put up that gun! What a big brave bastard you are—*now* you're willing to shoot him, but when he was robbing the bank, where the hell were you? Sam, Enos, Alf, make that simpleton put away that gun, then fetch a stretcher, and blast you, be quick about it!'

The crowd stirred a little, a thin-faced, wispy man, gun clutched in one hand, was shoved out through. Frank recognized the man—he was a part-time bar-tender—and ignored him as he walked on around the crowd in the direction of the bank.

Two cowmen, armed with saddleguns, were blocking the bank doorway. They nodded curtly and moved aside for Frank to enter. This was the first inkling Frank had that the Bivouac tragedy had not begun and ended out in the roadway. The banker, a portly, greying, rosy-cheeked man, was lying in a puddle of blood too.

A wilted, numb, older man was sitting upon a bench staring blankly. Behind him, the door to the bank's vault hung by one twisted steel hinge, and through the opening Frank could see all he had to see; the safe was a shambles. Greenbacks lay scorched, torn, crumpled and ripped apart amid the debris, but the main steel box inside the vault was yawning wide open—totally empty. It was in this second steel box where the cash was kept.

Frank, along with many other cowmen, and a number of local townsmen, had been cleaned out. The few ruined notes lying in the debris could not possibly

68

total up to more than a few hundred dollars.

The man on the bench turned his head very slowly to put glazed eyes upon Frank. 'Where is Mr Templer?' he whispered.

Frank did not reply, he simply moved back so that the old clerk could see the man in the pool of blood. *That* had been Mr Templer, manager and president of Bivouac's Stockman's Trust & Savings Company.

Frank returned to the roadway just in time to hear the cat-calling crowd berate Matthew Severns as the old man marched along behind the stretcher with the unconscious outlaw upon it.

Frank's attention was diverted when a crowd of horsemen whirled away from the southward livery-barn, all of them armed and several of them shaking carbines in upraised fists very melodramatically. The posse lunged across the main roadway and left only high dust in its wake as it raced eastward beyond town.

Frank went over to the front of Doc's building, shouldered through the crowd, banged on the door until Doc opened up, glaring fiercely, then Frank walked past and turned to say, 'A town-posse has gone out, Doc, and maybe they'll get lucky, but my personal feeling is that our only chance is through the man you've got in here . . . They cleaned out the bank vault neat as a bare rock. Did you have any money over there, Doc?'

Instead of replying the medical practitioner stamped past and jerked his head for Frank to follow along.

Chapter Eight

A DYING STRANGER

The unconscious outlaw was not a particularly large man although because he was bundled inside a riding coat, a woollen sweater and a heavy flannel shirt, he seemed to be large.

Also, he had curly dark hair and dark eyes, along with a weathered, sun-bronzed skin-tone which made him look possibly part Spanish, or part pale-Mexican.

In other parts of the country—for example, in upper New England, lying close to French Canada—people would have said he was perhaps French-Canadian, or possibly even Woodlands Indian despite his curly hair, but where he now was lying out flat, totally incapable of feeling anything, most dark skin-shadings were attributed to what was endemic to the Far West—Mex, Spanish, or perhaps even redskin.

All Doctor Severns had to say about the man's probable origin as he finished cutting away the sweater and shirt, was that wherever he came from, they must raise their share of stupid people, because from what Doc had heard, this wounded outlaw committed the unpardonable and inexcusable crime of tying his horse, then being unable to untie him in time to escape.

'It's not even ironic,' Doc said, snipping briskly with his scissors, 'it's stupid.'

The man had been hit three times, twice through the soft parts, once high on the right side. Doc gently removed the soggy clothing, tossed it aside, and leaned to squint at the little puckery holes. As he did this he explained. 'You look at wounds as though you could see under the skin. You know what lies in each area of the body, Frank, and what you do, is review in your mind's eye everything that bullet passed through on its way.' Doc pointed to the upper wound. 'Broken collarbone, out back, where the slug exited, but before it got out, it punctured the upper lobe of the lung.' Doc sighed and straightened back a little. 'It also caused hemorrhaging.' Doc went to a small table and put on a pair of eyeglasses over there, then he returned and pointed to the two lower wounds. 'These will kill him,' he said in a detached, impersonal tone. 'More hemorrhaging, of course, along with a ruptured spleen, torn arteries, punctured liver—and so forth.' Doc dropped the hand back to his side. 'Hand me that blue flask on the table, will you?'

Frank looked around, saw a blue bottle and handed it up. Doc pulled the cork, sniffed, made a grimace and raised the outlaw's head, poured some of the vile-smelling fluid down, then eased the man's head back. His next function was to fill a hypodermic syringe and shoot something directly into the man's bloodstream at the inner bend of one arm. Then he flapped his hands and removed the eyeglasses.

'He'll come around—with any luck—then perhaps he'll answer our questions, then he'll die, and there is no power on earth which can prevent that—his death, I mean.'

Doc looked at Frank. He was a man you did not argue with, and particularly about anything pertaining to his speciality, medicine.

Frank, looking at the handsome, bronzed face, said, 'He's young, Doc.'

Severns's answer was brusque. 'Men who die by violence usually are, Frank. You don't find men my age robbing banks.' Doc went to work removing all the man's upper clothing. The room was warm and well-lighted. The man's torso was well-muscled, his skin was paler where it had always been covered, and there was a simple golden wedding band upon his ringfinger. Doc did not miss that, either.

'Somewhere there is going to be a widow who don't even know she *is* one.' Doc frowned, then said, 'Remove whatever's in his pants pockets, Frank, while I go get us some coffee.' At the door he looked cynically back at the dying man. 'I've lived a long time, and I can tell you something I've observed over the years: Every man, in his lifetime, makes one total mistake. If he's lucky, he survives it. If he isn't lucky—well—*that* man tied a knot when he should only have looped his reins. It's a simple damned mistake, isn't it? Except that it killed this one.'

Doc left and Frank went to work emptying the man's pockets. There wasn't much; a clasp-knife,

72

some silver coins, a pressed-flat small packet of greenbacks in small denominations, a blue bandana handkerchief, a crumpled bit of paper which could have been a note or a letter, and a piece of yellow beeswax, the kind harness-makers used to pull thread through before they threaded sewing needles. The beeswax intrigued Frank, who had used many a ball of the stuff in his early youth.

When Doc returned with two cups of black coffee and looked at the motionless outlaw, Frank showed him the ball of beeswax. 'Harness-maker's equipment,' Frank said. Doc was not especially interested. He handed Frank a cup, then went to lean and gently lift an eyelid with his free hand.

'He'll be coming around soon.'

Doc stepped back, sipping coffee and watching the dying man. If he had any feelings of compassion they did not show in his vinegary old lined and weathered countenance. But he might have been feeling *something*, because he said, 'He won't feel pain. I shot enough laudanum into him to block everything.'

They stood waiting. When the outlaw slowly opened his eyes, Doc put down his coffee cup and stepped in close. 'You're hard hit,' he told the dark-eyed man. 'I'm a doctor and I've done what I can. You'll rest easy, but you don't have a whole lot of time, young man.'

The dark eyes moved slowly from Doc to Frank, then around the small, lighted room with its drawn shades and its clean walls and tables. They came back

73

to Doc and the man formed a question, which he seemed to have trouble uttering.

'What happened—afterwards?'

Doc pursed his lips as though something were inhibiting him, and frowned. 'You didn't make it, that's all. You got shot down in the roadway. The other men got away.'

Frank understood. For some private reason, Doc could not bring himself to tell the dying outlaw that he was lying there because of something stupid he had done. Maybe Doc did not want the dying man to realize the futility of his death.

Doc said, 'Who were they—the other bank-robbers; who were they?'

The dying man's dark eyes did not leave Doc's face although the man made no attempt to reply. There was no question about his understanding the question; he understood it, he just was not going to answer it.

Doc said, 'Listen to me, son. I've seen thousands of men die and I still only know one thing about death: It's not a curse; it's probably a wonderful experience—but don't do it without trying to be honest with those of us who are doing all we can to help you . . . Who were they?'

The outlaw's eyes rolled up around, and came to rest upon Frank, standing close behind Doc. 'You— the law?'

Frank answered quietly. 'No. The constable died out front of his jailhouse. I'm a cowman. I just rode into town.'

Doc picked up his coffee cup and held it without lifting it to his lips, watching the outlaw's face closely. 'What is your name?' he asked. 'You're a married man. That much we know. Don't leave your woman to wonder whatever became of her man. Be honest, son. You only have this one chance.'

The outlaw's lips moved gently, and fading words came softly into the silent room. 'I won't tell you who they were, but . . .

Doc leaned, still clutching his coffee cup, then he swore. 'Gawdammit, he's gone.'

Frank leaned to stare intently at the outlaw's chest. It had stopped its faint movement altogether.

Someone out front thumped the roadside door with a heavy fist, and Doc stepped back only after the knocking had been repeated three times, then he stalked out of the room, still holding the coffee cup, leaving Frank with the dead man.

When Doc returned he looked irritable. 'Sam,' he growled. 'Sam Leverett; he said they want this feller out in the roadway. I told him they can have him, but he's dead, so they'll have to lynch a corpse.'

Doc put aside the coffee cup and went over to poke through the effects Frank had mounded upon a little white table. Doc's irritability was understandable, and Frank's own feeling of frustration was sympathetic. Without looking back, Doc said, 'Pull a blanket over him.' Doc continued to rummage through the things on the table. He picked up the flat little packet of money, counted it, tossed it down and picked up the crumpled piece of paper and very painstakingly smoothed it out atop the table, then retrieved his glasses, settled them upon his nose, low down, and leaned to read the wording.

He removed his glasses, polished them furiously, replaced them and leaned to scan the crumpled paper again. Finally, he blew out a big ragged breath and turned to gaze at the blanket-shrouded corpse.

'Fine,' he said, flatly. 'Just damned fine.' He held out the crumpled paper. 'Frank.'

As the younger man accepted the paper Doc growled irritably. 'Never mind all that—just read the signature on the back . . . Ella Leland.'

Frank's head shot up, but Doc was glowering at the shrouded silhouette, so Frank took the letter to the lamp and read it—signature first, then the contents. It was Ella's announcement that she would be leaving Ohio the first of the month, and according to the stage schedules, she and John should arrive in Moab three weeks later. Otherwise, there was a brief paragraph about her pregnant condition, and the note closed with a wistful sentence about how things would certainly improve as soon as they were all together again.

Then her name in clear, firm script: Ella Leland.

Doc looked over at Frank, sardonically. 'Now what?' he asked. 'Frank, the older I get the less any of it makes sense to me. Him—no one forced him to be an outlaw—but *her*; what has *she* done to deserve what's ahead for her? . . . You ever read much about the Law of Retribution, things like that?'

Frank was only half-listening.

'I don't believe in it,' stated Doc, firmly. 'You know why? I'll tell you: Even if you assume *she's* done something bad, sometime—what in hell has that little baby-boy ever done? Nothing! He's not old enough to even hold his head up, much less commit some kind of damned crime—spiritual crime or any other kind. So—what sense does it make, any of it?'

Frank looked again at her signature, then glanced at the table where her husband lay dead. 'He was a miner, Doc.'

Matthew Severns nodded. 'That explains one thing, anyway—why the fool *tied* his horse, instead of just looping the reins. Miner or not, though, he was also a bank-robber.' Doc looked into his coffee cup, found a little black liquid still in it, and hoisted the cup to drain it, then he went to a cupboard, dug for a bottle of rye whiskey, and drank two big swallows of that as well, and handed the bottle to Frank.

'Drink,' he ordered. 'Right now, it's medicine, so drink.'

Frank obeyed and handed back the bottle. 'Doc, you'll have to explain this to her.'

Doc whirled. 'Me! I didn't take her in, Frank. I didn't deliver her child. I'm not her friend, *you* are. You're the only person in the country who's been her friend.'

'I can't do that, Doc.'

'Well now, by gawd, if you can't, Frank, who else will?'

77

Frank and the old man looked steadily at one another. Doc picked up the bottle of rye whiskey and took down two more swallows, then set the bottle back down, hard. 'You want to know something about me, Frank?' he snapped. 'My mother always said I should have been a minister of the Gospel, and my paw always said I should have been a banker. But my wife used to say the Lord called me to medicine because He knew I'd do my best to hold life here on earth, and when I lost it, I'd suffer like a martyr . . . You know who was right? All right; I'll drive out and tell her, but I'm going to do it in my own damned way.' Doc looked down at the bottle, as though he might reach for it again, but he didn't. Instead, he said, 'You stay right here in town until I get back, otherwise I won't do it. Agreed?'

Frank nodded his head, and reached for the bottle.

Outside, the town had turned quiet, the sun was high, all the dust had settled, and down at the log jail-house there were women in the milling crowd.

The talk of lynching had died when the saloon-owner, Sam Leverett, had reported what Doc had told him about the wounded outlaw dying. Generally, people had said about all there was to say. Now, all they could do was wait until someone rode back from the posse which had raced out of town, with news.

By the time Frank left Doc's place, the town was recovering from its initial shock, and was now turning silent and stunned. He went over to the saloon for a drink without anyone calling to him, even though

78

most of the people who saw him crossing the road knew he had been inside with Doc. People looked at him, steadily, and acted dumbstruck.

Chapter Nine

A LONG DAY ENDS

The saloon was a large room, decorated over the back-bar with several mounted trophy-heads of elk, deer, wapiti, and a huge, flat-faced black bear. It was unlike many cow-country saloons in that its bar was mahogany, its card tables were polished, and there was a solid floor of fir planking. The place had a look, and an atmosphere, of substance and orderliness.

The barman was a stranger to Frank Kandelin. Sam Leverett, the barrel-chested man who owned the place and who usually manned his own bar, was not present. In fact, excepting Frank and the youthful, impassive bartender, there were only six or eight other men in the room, which was understandable; what had just happened in Bivouac had never happened before. There had been gunfights and even a few holdups, but Bivouac was generally a peaceful, orderly town, and no one had ever attempted to rob the bank before. People were outside in the roadway in droves, but only a few men were inside the saloon when Frank got his drink and leaned there, sipping it, gazing at the big back-bar wall-clock, and feeling like the worst coward imaginable—except that he simply could not have ridden home to that beautiful woman and told her. Feeling cowardly was an excruciating experience, but the other feeling would have been infinitely worse.

He turned when a large man leaned along the bar at his side, and said, 'Was he pretty badly shot up?'

The large man was saloon-owner Sam Leverett. Frank answered succinctly. 'Bad enough, Sam. Two through the guts and one slug up high, through a lung. He didn't even have enough time to tell us his name—if he'd meant to.'

Leverett shook his head at the hovering barman. 'You know how much they got out of the bank?' he asked Frank. Then answered his own question. 'Nine thousand dollars.'

Frank finished his drink and shoved the little glass aside. 'Three thousand of it was mine. I just put it in; still got the receipt in my pocket.'

'I lost one thousand,' said the large man, bitterly. 'I hope to hell the posse catches the other ones.'

Frank nodded over that. He hoped so too.

Leverett said, 'We got to find a new constable.'

Frank remained silent. This was not his concern. He still hadn't overcome his feelings about the loss of Bert.

'Any ideas?' asked the saloonman.

Frank scowled. 'Hell no. That's for you folks in town to figure out.'

'Yeah, but you'd know if there was a gun-handy rider among the cow outfits, Frank. That's where we got Bert. That's about the only place where we can find someone suitable. There's sure as hell no one in town who could do the job.'

Frank remained indifferent. 'You'll find someone,' he murmured. 'When'll you bury Bert?'

'Tomorrow. I made the arrangements, and set a carpenter to making the coffin. Doggone it but I'm going to miss him. Bert was one of those fellers who could walk in here when I was being bothered by drunk rangeriders, and just look at them. He never once used a gun in here. That kind of a town marshal's not easy to come by.'

Frank paid for his drink, nodded to Sam Leverett, and walked back into the bright sunshine, heading for the liverybarn. The hostler down there told him Doctor Severns had left town a half hour earlier.

The liveryman walked over. He was a narrow-faced Texan with a nice smile and slightly crafty expression. Right now, his curiosity made that expression sharper as he said, 'You was up at Doc's wasn't you, Frank, when that bank-robber give up the ghost?'

Frank nodded.

'What's his name?' asked the liveryman. 'I was at Bert's office lookin' through all them wanted dodgers he had up there, tryin' to find someone who'd fit his description, and I found a slew of them, but they was all so much alike a feller'd need a name to figure one from the other.'

Frank did not lie, but neither did he tell the entire truth. He answered about as he'd done with Sam Leverett, except that with Sam he'd volunteered the information before Leverett had asked for it. He said, 'The man died without telling us his name. In fact, Doc was trying to get him to name his friends, the other bank-robbers, when he upped and died on us.'

The liveryman looked crestfallen. 'Sure would have he'ped,' he muttered. 'There's rewards on most of them old boys.'

Frank gazed at the sly-faced Texan, feeling disgust, then he walked down where his horse was looking from a stall, led the animal forth and cuffed him. The hostler went after Frank's saddle and bridle, but the liveryman drifted away, probably considering other methods of identifying the dead outlaw in the hopes of putting in a claim for the reward. One of the advantages of a whole town shooting at a man who subsequently died from multiple gunshot wounds, was that while most men would be reticent about even admitting they had been out there shooting at the solitary remaining outlaw over in front of the bank, one man like the Texan could claim he had killed the outlaw, and no one could really prove otherwise—and most people would not even challenge the claim.

Frank rode out the back way heading in the general direction of home, but he rode slowly, and stopped twice, once to water his horse at a fordable little white-water creek, and the second time when he topped a low roll of grassland and saw a band of cattle strung out on the far side, grazing.

He sat a long while studying the cattle. They belonged to him and they were slicking off, turning shiny, even the older cows which were still suckling big, sassy fat calves.

There were two bulls with the band, the younger of which picked up man- and horse-scent immediately, and came around with his horned head held high, ready to fight. He had a thick neck, the mark of the breeding and fighting season. Frank smiled and did not move, did nothing which would aggravate the young bull. Eventually, the animal tired of his vigil and went back to grazing. Then Frank turned out and rode far around the herd so as to cause no disturbance. *Cowmen* never deliberately choused their cattle; every time fat cattle ran they sweated off weight. *Cowboys* might be that thoughtless, but not *cowmen*.

He had the ranch in sight by mid-afternoon, and also two of his riders loping towards home from off in the distant northwest. It was still early. He watched them, remembering what Curtis had said about cowboys who are too well fed, then shrugged and headed on in, too.

The yard was empty when he had it fully in sight, which meant that Doc had been and gone. This made him uneasy. Now, he would have to face Ella alone.

Curtis walked out front, between the shoeing-shed and the log barn when he saw Frank coming, and leaned upon the tie-rack molding a cigarette, clearly awaiting Frank's arrival. Those other two riders, Slim and Tomahawk, had passed from sight out behind the barn. Otherwise, there was no one around as Frank rode up, swung off, and nodded at his rangeboss.

Curtis said, 'Doc was here.'

Frank yanked loose his latigo without commenting. Until he was lugging the saddle inside to its peg he did not speak, but as he draped the rig by one stirrup, he said, 'Yeah, I know. Did you talk to him?'

Curtis had. 'Out front of the mainhouse.' Curtis did not enter the barn because he was smoking, but he stood just short of the opening as he talked to Frank. 'That was a hell of a thing. Just dynamiting the bank and killing old Templer, was a hell of a thing. And Bert.'

Frank strolled back out into the failing daylight of late afternoon, and looked to his right where Slim and Tomahawk were freeing horses into the corral.

'Did you talk to Doc after he told Miz' Leland?'

Curtis hadn't. 'No. He told me what he was out here for, though, and he was inside with her for more'n an hour . . . I didn't much want to be around when he come out, so I was over in the wagon-shed, and watched him drive off. He didn't look very happy, Frank.' Curtis dropped his smoke and ground it underfoot. 'I'm glad you're back, though. Seems to me she'd need someone besides her lad—someone grown up and all. I worked for a feller once, when I was first starting out, who rolled a wagon on himself, and that's the first time I ever saw a woman come apart . . . I'd just as soon never have to see that again.'

Frank faced in the direction of the mainhouse and figuratively hauled up and stiffened his resolve. 'I never did this before, either,' he admitted, then turned and started across the yard.

Over at the corrals, Tomahawk and Slim broke the late-day soft quiet with laughter, and came ambling around from the corrals where Curtis looked stonily at them, then jerked his head and stalked down inside the barn. Tomahawk and Slim exchanged a bewildered look, then followed Curtis inside.

The mainhouse was silent, which it probably should have been, but when Frank climbed both wide steps to the long porch and pushed past the door, he rather thought he would hear wailing, or at the very least, sobbing. He heard nothing. Nor was there any sign of Ella or John.

He stood a while in the parlor uncertain of his role, then headed for the cookshack and some coffee—and came face to face with her, out there, dry-eyed, stony-faced, methodically slicing meat while John was peeling potatoes over a large, dented old pan. John's dark eyes looked swiftly up, then brightened with warm acknowledgement, and two things struck Frank at the same time: The first thing was that Ella had not told John about his father. The second thing that stopped Frank in his tracks was that those dark, alert eyes were identical with the eyes of the dead bank-robber. Now Frank knew where the lad had got his dark eyes and dark hair.

Ella saw him, reached for a towel to dry her hands

upon, and said, 'Son, you go right ahead with the potatoes, Mister Kandelin and I'll be out back.' Then she
turned and led the way, without another glance at
either of them.

Frank smiled at the lad, winked, and followed Ella
out into the sweet-scented, cooling late-day shadows,
behind the house where great trees cast shade and
shadows, and where all the perfume of wildflowers
and flourishing grass and underbrush permeated the
utterly still, warm air.

She stopped in shadows and turned to face him, and
what he had dreaded most, was lacking: She was dry-
eyed. 'I am grateful that Doctor Severns drove out,'
she said, looking directly up into Frank's face. 'He—
you wouldn't think to look at him, that he could be so
gentle. I'm very grateful to him, Mister Kandelin . . .
And to you; he told me how you were there, willing to
do all you could to save Mike.'

Frank kept his features completely impassive. He
had not done anything at all, but stand there. He
hadn't known what to do; it had all been Doc's drama.

She clasped both hands across her stomach,
knuckles showing white against the dark blue of her
cotton dress. He waited, but when she stood silently
for a while, he said, 'Well; everything will be done for
him, Miz' Leland. Tomorrow. I'll go in first, then
Curtis can drive you and John and the baby in. I'll
have the boys clean up the wagon.'

Her chin whitened, but that was all. Her intensely
blue eyes were as dry as before. 'Mister Kandelin—I

thought there might be something like this. Well—he sent us money, but his letters rarely mentioned mining, and there was something else—not just some little articles I saw in the newspapers back home, but—Mike. Mister Kandelin, I *knew* my husband. I told you he was a restless man. That wasn't the whole of it. He was also wayward. There were little things in his past, and even after we were married, there were incidents.'

Frank shifted stance. 'You don't have to tell me any of this, ma'am.'

'Yes I do. You're the *one* person I have to tell.'

'Ella, you don't owe me anything. Not a blessed thing. I haven't done anything most folks wouldn't have done, and I didn't do anything I didn't want to do.'

She stared at him. 'Well then, Frank, may I tell you anyway?'

It finally came to him that she *wanted* to talk to him, that she *had* to talk, so he smiled, reached for one of her hands and led her along the rear of the log house to a place where there was an old log bench bolted to a cottonwood tree, and he sat her down over there, sank down beside her and pushed out his legs in the pleasant and silent shade.

'Mining is a thankless occupation,' he said quietly. 'They're in mud and muck most of the day, either cold or boiling hot.'

'But they don't all turn to robbing banks, do they?'

He did not answer.

'Frank; it was the baby. I had an idea that the baby would make things different. He was fond of John, so he would have been fond of the new baby, and with *two* little boys . . . But a friend of mine back home told me once that nothing changes a mature man from whatever he basically is, and now, you see, she was right.' Ella turned slightly to look at Frank in the shadows. 'Maybe you don't know this, but love between two people doesn't just go on and on and on, Frank; it either grows or it doesn't grow. One person by themself can't make it do that; they *both* have to work at it.'

He didn't know, but it sounded reasonable, so he gently inclined his head, still saying nothing.

'I told you how frightened and alone I felt crossing that big desert the other day, coming up here from Fort Sunday. Well; it wasn't just the desert, it was something else: Suppose I couldn't make it work, up at Moab? Suppose it got worse instead of better, and I had the two children to look after in a strange, rough place, with no money and no friends?'

She folded her hands and leaned back, looking westerly, beyond the house out across the evening-mantled grasslands. 'And it didn't work, did it?' she murmured. 'Frank; I didn't know what to say or what to think—or even what to feel—when Doctor Severns told me . . . But I know now. It wouldn't have worked, but at least this way, the pain came all at once, instead of being dragged out for a miserable year . . . I'll ride in tomorrow and bury Mike, then I'll go back home.'

Chapter Ten

DIFFERENT PEOPLE,
DIFFERENT REACTIONS

When he was out front of the bunkhouse in the late evening with Curtis, explaining about taking Ella and the children to town for the funeral in the morning, he told his rangeboss something else.

'A man knows things happen, Curt, and he expects them to happen, and when they do, well hell, if there's nothing he can do, he accepts them. Maybe they hurt a man or haunt him, but there it is—they happen, and he can't do much about it, so he does a lot of quiet thinking, and figures out what has to come next, then he goes ahead and does what he's got to do.'

Curtis nodded and eyed the tip of his burning cigarette.

'*She's* like that, Curt. She's soft like womenfolk should be, but at the same time she sees right to the heart of things. I never knew a woman who thought like a man, before, did you?'

Curtis hadn't, but then he hadn't ever been much of a hand with women; like most rangeriders, he occasionally frequented the 'hog ranches'—the houses of prostitution to be found in almost every cow-town—but he had never had a genuine attachment, and had never sought one. But he'd known ranch-women, so he said, 'Seems to me she's pretty young to be tough-minded, though, but yeah, I've know older women at the camps and ranches who thought like their men-folk.' He eyed Frank a thoughtful moment. 'What happens to her now?'

'She said she'd bury her husband, then head back to Ohio.'

Curtis didn't think much of that. 'Damned shame,' he mumbled, then changed the subject. 'We'll have the wagon ready right after breakfast, come morning.'

They strolled down to the corral before Curtis mentioned something he and the riders had privately discussed. 'How much did they get out of the bank?'

'Nine thousand dollars.'

Curtis, like most rangemen, had never actually seen more than two or three hundred dollars at one time in their lives, and was flabbergasted. 'Lord a'mighty.'

'Three thousand of it was from the drive last fall,' said Frank, hooking a booted foot upon a corral stringer and leaning pensively to gaze in at the drowsing saddle-stock. 'If they don't find those fellers, we'll be hurting before next summer.'

'What are they doing—with Bert dead?'

'Town-posse went out,' explained Frank. 'Looked like a band of schoolboys chasing coyotes.'

Curtis leaned, also, and looked at the indifferent horses. 'Town-posse aren't any good,' he stated. 'Soft men riding soft horses.'

Frank wasn't that disparaging, but he did not have

much faith in town-posse either, so he said, 'Sam Leverett lost a thousand dollars, and I'd expect some of the other stockmen probably lost about that much, which means the whole countryside'll be roiled up. I'd guess those bastards won't get clean away; everyone was up in arms before they got clean away from town. The hue and cry'll be taken up all across the territory.' He turned. 'If Leland was one of them, then my guess is that he wasn't the only miner from Moab among them. That ought to make it easier to track them down.'

Curtis dryly said, 'Not leanin' on a corral like we're doing, Frank. Suppose I take Tomahawk with me to the funeral tomorrow. He can lead my saddle horse behind the wagon, and as soon as it's over at the graveyard, him and me can sort of just drift off and go manhunting.'

Frank considered this, and decided it would do no harm, and just might do some good. 'Then you'd better take Simon along to fetch Ella and the kids back,' he said, and hauled upright off the corral. 'Ask around town before you ride out; some of those possemen will sure have returned. They'd ought to know which way the tracks led.'

Together, they strolled back to the bunkhouse, and parted there. The mainhouse was lighted, but not in the parlor; out back where Ella's bedroom was. Frank entered through the cookshack so as not to make any noise, and went to his own room, which was off the small, cluttered room he used for the ranch office, and

91

as he got ready to bed down he softly heard the baby crying. It sounded more like cranky wailing than a genuine cry. He went to bed listening to that sound, and had troubled slumber.

Dawn was only beginning to brighten the eastern world when Frank met the riders out front of the bunkhouse. Curtis had already explained about the trip to town, so Simon was wearing his leather cuffs and his clean blue shirt, things he only wore upon special occasions, while Tomahawk looked as he always looked, except for *his* clean shirt. Slim, who would remain at the ranch, was dressed for work, except that he had shed his spurs, and that meant he would be working close to the sheds or the corrals.

He volunteered to go make coffee and start the fatback to frying for breakfast. None of them expected Ella to be in the cookshack this morning, but when Slim got over there, she already had a fresh pot of coffee on the stove, and was heating a raisin pudding. Slim was at a loss, so he stood in the doorway, hat in hand, until she saw him, and smiled perfunctorily at him. Then he came forward to help, and she asked if he'd go on through the house and help John get dressed. She looked Slim in the eye and said, 'I told him what happened yesterday, and why we are going into town today, Slim. He's still a little boy.'

Slim's answer was short. 'I know, ma'am. I went through this when I was his age, or close to it.' He walked away heading for the parlor door.

The other men finished what had to be done at the

barn, then trooped to the cookshack and were met by their breakfast meal already two-thirds through the process of preparation. They solemnly greeted Ella, and no one tried to force conversation. None of them asked where Slim was. Right at this moment the stove could have disappeared and they would not have said a word about it, but, like all men who know perfectly well what it is like to force an extra ounce of service out, when such forcing amounts to a near impossibility, they appreciated Ella very much.

Curtis, watching her work, drifted a slow gaze around to Frank, and without uttering a word they exchanged a conviction. She was not only as realistic and tough-minded as a man—hell—she was also as physically, resolutely, tough.

When the meal was finished and the men marched back outside, Frank turned in the doorway, the last one out, and spoke across the room, softly.

'The rig will be ready directly, Ella. Whenever you're ready . . . You didn't have to do any of this.'

She kept her back to him, working near the stove, when she replied. 'I told John . . . I had to tell him. This is going to be very hard on him, Frank.'

There was no doubt about that, but Frank was thinking of *her*, not her son. It would be much harder on *her*. John's anguish would be only part of *her* anguish; the entire burden lay squarely upon her.

But he could not think of the correct words to express his feelings, nor his thought, so all he said was: 'Folks will understand.'

Now, she turned to face him. 'Will they?' she demanded. 'We're strangers. John's father was killed trying to rob their bank, and Doctor Severns said the banker was killed as well as the constable. Why should the people down there feel anything but terrible resentment towards my sons and me, Frank?'

He gazed steadily at her. *This* was a part of her burden he hadn't even thought about.

Her face was white and drawn, the blue eyes very dark. Aside from the ordeal of giving birth, up at the top of the pass, all these other things were riding her spirit. He stood looking back at her, beginning to realize that she was a very rare individual. But even rare individuals had a point beyond which they could not force themselves.

He wished he dared suggest that she stay home today, but he knew better than to mention it. She knew what her duty was, evidently, and if it killed her, or if she collapsed finally, she would do what she considered her obligation.

The only thing he could think of to say, was: 'What *he* did, Ella, you're not responsible for.' Then, as he turned to follow after his men, he also said, 'I wish this day was over.'

The sun was climbing beyond the farthest rims, the men had the rig outside, with the team being harnessed to it, and as Frank passed around the corner of the house he saw Slim and the boy on the front veranda. John was scrubbed and dressed in a clean shirt and a rusty black coat. He was wearing a cap, something which was probably appropriate back in Ohio, but which was something one rarely saw west of the Missouri River.

The boy's face was locked down in a set expression of stoniness. Frank thought of a similar expression upon the face of John's mother, and decided that whatever John's father had been, the lad had got his iron from Ella. Then he walked on down where Simon and Tomahawk were snaking out a pair of saddle-animals.

There was very little warmth in the yard, yet, although sunlight shone brilliantly. The men were moving with the customary stiffness of early morning, and adding to that was their silence and their unsmiling expressions.

Ella came from the house, carrying the bundled baby, as the men in the barn led forth their animals. Only Slim stood aside, after boosting John into the wagon-bed and giving him a rough slap on the shoulder.

Simon, in his elegant leather cuffs, riding the best horse in his string, looked like a bronzed centaur. It was something Simon Bowers shared with most Apaches; he looked, and actually was, awkward, bandy-legged and physically out of proportion on the ground, but in the saddle he was graceful and even handsome.

Curtis handed Ella up, then took his seat and flipped the lines. Slim leaned on the tie-rack gazing after them, and finally, a thin kind of increasing warmth came into the new day.

The trip to Bivouac was middling-long under almost any circumstances, even on a saddle-horse, but in a wagon it dragged interminably, its only saving grace the beauty of the springtime countryside. The trees, carpeting miles of emerald grass, wildflowers, and the cloud-speckled azure heavens, worked in unison to soften the hardest soul and salve the rawest spirit. They had been traveling for two miles in dogged silence when Curtis looked around, saw the baby's partially exposed face, and smiled at Ella.

'Sure goin' to be a fine boy, ma'am. I worked for an outfit up in the Cache Le Poudre country of Wyoming one summer, and the lady up there had a boy looked enough like this one to be his twin brother. Before I left, he was hiking around, no bigger'n a minute, getting into more mischief than it seemed a little kid could even figure out, let alone get into.'

Ella's stone-steady, dead-ahead-gaze did not break away for a moment, but eventually it did. She smiled slightly at Curtis. She did not want to talk and she did not want to smile, but he was trying hard to help.

'Do you like children?' she asked him, and Curtis turned back to studying the rhythmically-rising rumps of the team while he pondered that before replying. He had been around children, of course, but he had always had a somewhat detached interest in them. They had never been *his* children, and at best he would only be around them one or two riding seasons, so he never became very involved. After he had tried, without complete success, to define his feelings, he answered slowly.

'Well; most folks have to start out by being one, and there's plenty to be said in favor of 'em. But only boys. No offense meant, ma'am.'

Ella's blue gaze lingered on Curtis's weathered, lean profile for a while. He was a Westerner; in time she would understand Westerners, but so far all she really knew about the ones she'd encountered, was that they had a casual, good-natured approach to life which included a natural involvement with other people's troubles. They were also generous, in the same casual manner, as though these things were binding upon them; as though, in their raw environment, the need for people to aid one another were something everyone just naturally understood, and complied with.

She faced forward again, watching the golden sunlight splash out its burnished brilliance down-country in the direction of Bivouac.

She was drawing strength from Curtis, and from the other men riding with her. It was a wonderful comfort. She looked at her newborn son, tucked the blanket closer even though it was no longer chilly, then she twisted to look at her other son. He was also watching the countryside roll past, but when their eyes met, he did not smile, which was something John ordinarily did readily and easily. He was almost thirteen years old, and today was the first day of his manhood. She felt a pang of sadness for him; he should have been able to be a little boy for at least another year or two.

Chapter Eleven

A CHANGE IN PLANS

Frank left them at the outskirts of town to take the spare horse Curtis would ride, later, on down to the liverybarn. Simon loped with him.

The liveryman was not on hand, but his dayman was. He took their animals, and casually mentioned that he had just returned from the funeral for the constable and Philip Templer, then he said, 'They're going to bury that outlaw after dinner, but I sure don't know who's going to be out there. Sam said they'd ought to cart him up a canyon and leave him for the wolves.'

Simon, after a sharp glance at his employer, spoke swiftly. 'We want these here animals cuffed down, grained, and stalled. They'll be getting some riding after a while.'

The dayman nodded. 'I'll take care of it.' He still had one more comment to make, probably because something besides horses was uppermost in his mind. 'Sam's going to send down to the U.S. Marshal's office for a deputy to come up and sit in until we can get another constable.'

Frank frowned over that. U.S. Deputy Marshals did not perform any such function that he had ever heard of. He and Simon left the barn, then paused out front in soft sunshine and tree-shade. Simon sighed. 'They won't know who she is, until after the funeral, and if folks don't turn up for the burying, it'll be better all around. I'll go find Curt and Tomahawk.'

Frank was agreeable to that. 'See if you can find a decent place for Miz' Leland to sit, while she's waiting.'

As Simon wobbled away, his bandy-legs carrying that thick, mighty torso as though they were overburdened, Frank gazed up in the direction of Leverett's saloon. Evidently Sam had either assumed the role of local leader, or had been pushed into it, but either way he would probably be the best man to talk to about what the posse had turned up, so Frank walked up there. On the way he nodded to people he had known for years, and had only seen once or twice before in all that time, dressed in ties and suit-coats. Apparently two funerals in one day had occupied just about everyone.

There were several cow-horses at the tie-rack in front of Sam's place when Frank got up there, and pushed on past the louvred doors. The cowmen ranged loosely along the bar, were also spruced up. At least their hats had been brushed, their boots freshly oiled, and their shirts were fresh. Their attendance at the twin funerals was not surprising. Most of them had patronized the bank, and every rider in the country had been acquainted with Bert. Also, there was the matter of the robbery, and this was what they were all quietly discussing when Frank entered, and received several solemn nods as he strode to the bar.

Sam Leverett came down his bar, and leaned, his strong face and bold eyes showing candid curiosity about something.

Frank said, 'Whiskey.'

Leverett got the bottle, and brought back two glasses. He poured Frank's glass full, first, then the second glass, which he cupped a big hand around as he leaned and said, 'I was talking to Doc last night, down at the liverybarn.'

Frank looked steadily at the larger and older man while he tasted the whiskey. He did not say a word, but he had a sinking sensation behind his belt-buckle.

'Frank; that lady you delivered the baby for—the one you taken in out at the ranch. . . .'

'Yeah? What about her? I brought her to town this morning, Sam. Her and my riders.'

Leverett considered the glass in his fist without making a move to raise it. 'Is she really that son of a bitch's wife?'

Frank put aside his half-empty shot-glass before replying. 'She *was* his wife.' He felt like cursing Doc Severns. 'Sam; she's a *woman*. She's got two small kids. That—son of a bitch—is dead. How would things look to you, if you were in her boots?'

Leverett stood staring at the whiskey-glass for a moment before speaking again. 'You're takin' her side?' he eventually asked, raising hard, bold eyes.

Frank's color came up slowly. 'What the hell are you talking about—her side? She had no idea what her husband's been doing, except that he wrote her back in Ohio he was mining up around Moab.'

'Yeah,' sneered Leverett. 'Well, maybe you just got to town, so I'll tell you something: We heard from the constable up at Moab by the morning stage, and *he* said Leland and three other worthless bastards have been raiding and robbing since last winter. They don't have any rewards out on them, yet, but he also said the U.S. Marshal's after them for stopping a couple of mail stages.'

Frank stared steadily at the saloonman. 'Sam—that was him, for Chriz' sake—not *her*, or those little boys.' Three of the nearby cowmen turned, taking an interest in what was being said. But they offered no comments, they simply stood there looking at Frank, and listening. Frank's irritability kept mounting.

'The man is dead,' he told the barman. 'I'll agree with anyone who figures he'd ought to be dead—but I brought her and the lads to town to see him off at the graveyard, Sam. Whatever Leland was, she was his wife, and it looks to me like she's doing what any decent woman would do . . . And Sam, if you come out there and do anything . . .' Frank reached for the bottle, carefully poured Leverett's glass full, then smiled as he shoved the bottle away. 'She's a stranger to everything we've got out here, and her whole lousy world caved in last night when Doc told her what had happened—and, she's got two little boys, no money, and damned little of anything else . . . . Drink your whiskey.' Frank settled a silver cartwheel on the bartop, turned and crossed the silent room, walked out into the fresh sunlight, and stood a moment looking up and down the roadway.

An older man, craggy, raw-boned, squint-eyed and wind-reddened, strolled forth behind him, smelling strongly of whiskey he'd been drinking at the bar. His name was Hal Underwood. He was one of the largest cowmen between the Carrizos and the Abajos. He said, 'What's on your mind, Frank? I mean after the buryin'.'

Frank turned. He adjoined old Underwood's range to the east. They had worked together, had been friends, for years. Frank knew Hal Underwood as a quiet, tough, unyielding man of powerful convictions and scrupulous honesty.

'After the burying,' he answered, 'I figure to try and get my three thousand dollars back. What's the story about the town-posse that went out yesterday?'

Underwood thinly smiled, stepped up and spat amber into the roadway dust, then softly said, 'They tracked 'em until suppertime, then some of them come back to town.' Underwood's narrowed, hard eyes showed hard humor. That was as near as he came to ridiculing the town-posse. Then he said, 'I sent my rangeboss and four men out to join them. There's some other outfits sent men along, too.'

'Which way are they riding?' asked Frank. The last he had seen of anyone concerned with the robbery, they had left town in a dead run, northeastward.

Underwood said, 'West.'

Frank blinked. 'Towards my range?'

'Yep.' Underwood's calm gaze did not waver. 'They'll head into the foothill range, I'd expect, but if they'd used their damned heads, they'd have held straight back up towards Moab. Better country to run over.' Underwood leaned to jettison another spume of tobacco juice before continuing. 'Don't seem to me they know this country down here—or else the others are as stupid as Leland was, and don't use their brains. Frank, they can't make good time through the hills, even if they get up there before someone finds 'em and pins them down.' The old man stared steadily at Kandelin. 'Don't worry about anyone going to the graveyard and lookin' mean at the lady. I'll go out there; me and four, five of the other fellers who was inside at the bar.'

Frank faintly frowned as the implication behind old Underwood's sardonic sentences soaked in. 'I'm going to be out there with her, Hal. Hell; I'm the only person around she—.'

'I just told you,' stated the dry old cowman. 'She's not going to be bothered. Not by Sam and not by anyone else . . . Frank, you know that country north of you better'n the In'ians knew it. My men sure don't know it. As for those clowns from town on their fat-

103

rumped horses—hell—they'll ride right up onto them men and we'll be havin' funerals around here for a month.' Underwood glanced up the roadway. 'Where's the lady?'

Frank knew where the wagon was. He told Underwood that much, then he also said Ella was with Curt, Simon and Tomahawk. Underwood nodded thoughtfully. 'Take your 'breed-In'ian with you, and maybe Curtis.'

Something like that had been Frank's original notion. He stood frowning. The idea of abandoning Ella right at this critical time, pained him. On the other hand, as Underwood had just said, he knew all that rough country north and west better than anyone around—and also, it was no rough guess to say townsmen, regardless of their good motivation, were not fair matches for fleeing, desperate, gun-handy renegades. If anything happened to the town-posse, Sam Leverett wouldn't be the only one fuming about Ella being Mike Leland's survivor. Dead men, in places like Bivouac, left kinsmen behind who never forgot, and did not very readily forgive, even though a dead outlaw hadn't actually been around to get involved in additional killings. And the little boys would have enough stigma to grow up with, to learn to live with, without piling on any more.

'Simon's to take her home right after the burying,' he told Underwood, then he thought of confronting Ella and telling her he wouldn't be there at her side, after all, and that made him wince.

The old, squint-eyed cowman's faded, hard eyes did not leave Frank. He laconically said, 'Go on down and get saddled up. I'll find Curtis and Tomahawk and send 'em along. Frank; you don't have no choice— unless you just want to back-slide,' and when the younger man's eyes flashed, Underwood sighed, unperturbed by rough anger, which he had faced countless times during his lifetime. 'I know you lost money in that robbery, too. Next summer, when you're sweatin' over operating funds, think back. Anyway, if she's any kind of a lady, she'll *know* what's got to be done . . . As for the rest, you don't have a blasted thing to worry about. Mark my word— Sam Leverett won't even walk out there. Neither will anyone else that means to act mean.' Underwood turned and glanced off in the direction of the town's upper end. 'I'll find 'em and send 'em along to the barn to you.' He walked away as calmly, as imperturbably, as he'd acted all along.

Frank turned southward, angled across the roadway, hitched at the gunbelt under his coat as he stepped up onto the yonder plankwalk, and was tormented by what he was doing all the way down to the liverybarn.

Even the dayman was not around, this time, so he had to get his own horse and lug out the saddle from a smelly harness-room. He was almost finished when Curtis and Tomahawk walked in, looking quizzical. The 'breed said nothing; he walked past Frank in search of his ranch-horse down the row of stalls, but

Curtis stopped and said, 'What's this all about? Old Underwood said they were on the northwest range, somewhere, but hell, that can't be right, Frank; they left out of town yesterday. By now they'd ought to be back to Moab—or somewhere just as far off.'

Frank did not dispute this. He simply said, 'Get saddled, Curt.' Then, at the look on his friend's face, he relented a little. 'Underwood said they went towards the foothills above our range. He got that from a posseman who returned to town last night. If they *did* go up in there, the chances are better than even that they'll be two or three more days getting through to the plains on the Moab side—on half-dead horses.'

Curtis stood his ground. 'And us?'

'I'll show you,' replied Frank. 'Now let's get the hell gone.'

Tomahawk never opened his mouth, until they were leading the animals out back, then he looked at Frank almost pityingly and spoke his thoughts. 'You're leavin' that lady at a mighty poor time.' That was all Tomahawk said. He sprang astride, evened-up his reins, and when his companions turned up the alleyway to the first opening which would allow them to cross over into open country, Tomahawk loped along, already beginning to narrow his gaze and consider the heat-hazed, far-distant slopes along the distant rim of the rolling grasslands above, and beyond, FK range.

Chapter Twelve

UPCOUNTRY

Curtis's opinion remained unchanged: With a twenty-four-hour head-start, excepting the possemen from town who had rushed out within minutes of the robbery, pursuit at this late date was unlikely to create a threat to the outlaws. He said, 'Hell; once they make it into the broken country, they could climb off and *lead* their animals, and still reach the open country on the far side, before we can get half-way across.'

Whether this was true or not, and it certainly seemed reasonable, they had the home-ranch in sight by the time Tomahawk came up with a pertinent observation. He had been riding along squinting towards the distant slopes for a couple of hours, off and on, obviously engrossed in private speculations.

'They camped last night,' he told Frank and Curtis. 'If them townsmen got any sense at all, they'd have been watching for the light above the treetops, and if they got just a little bit more sense, they pushed ahead last night and come in pretty close before dawnlight.'

Curtis snorted. 'You're giving a town-posse credit for more brains than it would have, Tomahawk. I've been out with a few like this one . . .' Curtis dolorously waggled his head to indicate total disillusionment.

Tomahawk said no more, but his expression underwent no change, so it was possible that he had not been deterred by Curtis's reasoning.

They did not ride to the ranch. It lay on their left, visible to the southwest as they loped diagonally across the miles-deep open grassland seeking to reach the foremost foothills before sundown. It seemed pointless to Curtis, to make good time, now, a day late, but he said little about it because Frank was beginning to react a little resentfully to his attitude.

They saw a horseman coming towards them, but a little more to the west, when they were within four of five miles of the initial broken-country, and fanned out a little to affect an interception.

The rider saw them sweeping towards him and halted stock-still. He then lifted out his carbine and sat balancing it across his lap, one-handed, while he continued to sit and wait. His horse was head-hung, so he could not have outrun them, which left him with only that one alternative: Wait and see who they were before doing whatever *that* required of him.

He was a youngish, sandy-haired, reddish-faced man who worked at the harness shop. The only name most folks knew him by was Herman. It could have been his first, or last, name; most likely his first name, though. When he finally recognized the trio of horsemen, he upended his Winchester and slid it back into the boot, then looped his reins and went to work fashioning a smoke. He had it lighted by the time those FK men walked their horses on up the last hundred or so yards. Herman blew smoke and said, 'You fellers ain't the only stockmen back up in there. Some fellers from old Underwood's outfit come in about an hour back, and they told me there was more stockmen on the way.'

Frank, eyeing the spent horse, asked an obvious question. 'You had enough, Herman?'

'No, but my horse has,' replied the sandy-haired man, looking pityingly at his mount. 'He just ain't used to this sort of thing.'

'None of them are,' muttered Curtis, 'that spend all week eating and loafing in a town corral.' Curtis looked past. 'How many possemen are still up there?'

Herman answered shortly. 'Three. Two went back last night—married fellers with wives that worry. This morning couple more left, then my horse plumb give out, so I had to turn back.' Herman twisted from the waist, looking back. 'I'll tell you gents something; that country'll fool you. I've never been back up in there before. I always figured it was sort of open and grassy and gentle, the way it is down here along the foothills. But it's a bastard. The farther in you go, the rougher it gets. Where I turned back we come onto an old In'ian village with a real good old saddlehorse-trail just west of it, up through a wide pass—but hell—by that time we was all ready to drop.' Herman straightened forward. 'That's where we spent the night—at that old dog-town.'

'How about the outlaws?' asked Tomahawk, and got a blank look from the saddlemaker.

'What about them?'

'Well—where did *they* spend the night?'

Herman looked mildly annoyed. 'Now how in hell would I know that? Farther up through the slopes, I reckon. Anyway, that's bad country—tough on saddlestock.'

Frank smiled. 'Hope you make it back all right. If you don't think your horse'll get you there, turn off at FK and borrow a fresh animal.' Frank reined around, lifted his horse over into a slow lope, and broke away with his companions, heading up the saddlemaker's back-trail, their only reliable set of tracks, so far.

Once, just before they entered the first segment of upended country, Tomahawk leaned and said, 'You fellers ever get the feeling the country's inhabited by nit-wits?'

Curtis and Frank laughed.

The lower foothills were friendly. Cattle frequently grazed up through here, although they never made a habit of remaining, because farther upcountry, where the forest-stands were, occasional cougar—and bear-scent came down on the light winds, and those were two scents cattle ran from awaiting a sighting.

The grass was flourishing. This far into new grazing season, FK had pushed no cattle up here, and Frank was the only cowman with an adjacency, so other stockmen did not graze over this far, all of which helped the feed situation.

In fact, the feed was so heavy they encountered some difficulty following Herman's sign. Even Tomahawk had to bend from his saddle as he led the way.

Beyond the gentler country, though, this westerly continuation of the Abajos was nowhere nearly as compatible as the easterly Abajos were. West of Bivouac, and of course miles northward of it, the terrain, once it passed up out of the grassy foothills, became heavily forested, shot through with lichen-speckled rock outcroppings, and the higher those three riders went, the more rough and inhospitable the terrain became.

There was still occasional Indian sign; not much of it, and after each winter there was less of it, but Tomahawk's affinity kept him pointing to things—dozens of ancient, sunken stone-rings, grass-filled old clearings where hideouts—and holdouts—had lived secretly. Crevasses where skeletons lay beneath tons of mounded stones, and now and then an overhead lattice, awaiting the next wind or snowfall to collapse and disintegrate, where the Indians had draped their thinly-sliced meat to dry in summer sunlight.

Tomahawk had only one comment to make about all this. 'They sure worked hard, living like that.' He shook his head in admiration, but not with envy.

From this point onward, Frank told Tomahawk to head farther west, and when the 'breed looked puzzled, Frank pointed off through the fragrant, shadowy forest. 'That trail Herman was talking about, near the uplands village-site, begins west of us, over about a mile. Six or eight years ago I stumbled across it when I was out elk hunting. I followed it to that village

111

Herman said the possemen camped at, last night, then on up through a slot, and without sweating my horse hardly at all, I reached the top-out and could see the Moab Plains on the far side.' He smiled. 'And *that's* what I had in mind when we left town; maybe we can't make up the lost time, but we sure as hell can make better advantage of this country, than those renegades would be able to, not knowing these mountains.'

Tomahawk paused only once, on the way to the horseback trail, and that was when he came upon the day-old tracks of horsemen riding bunched up. 'Posse,' he guessed. 'And under their tracks are maybe the tracks of them outlaws.'

It was possible. Frank simply said, 'Keep going.' When they were two-thirds of the way along, he also said, 'I think we can get them, now. They're going to hole up again tonight. We'll keep right on going, and with any kind of damned luck, we should be up to them, or maybe even a few miles ahead of them, come morning.'

Neither of his companions made a single comment. What Frank had implied was that they were not going to dismount all night long. Possemen, particularly town-possemen, yielded to weariness and darkness. Even those rangemen riding with the town-possemen, the ones old Underwood had sent out, might roll up around a fire tonight, and Frank had no doubt at all but that Mike Leland's partners would do that. Of all the riders in the mountains, now, the renegades were certainly the band most in need of a respite.

Finally, Tomahawk hauled up in a thin fringe of trees, then shoved back his hat and looked over at Frank. 'I never knew this trail was here, and hell, I've hunted a little up in here—but mostly more to the east, in the grassy country.'

They 'blew' their horses for a few minutes while talking, then turned northward. The trail was obviously very old. In places, where it crossed over rock-beds, it was worn as much as six to eight inches right down through solid stone. It took an awful lot of moccasins, over an awful lot of centuries, to accomplish that. Curtis and Tomahawk were impressed, not just at the 'find' but also at the obvious vast age of this trail.

It had undoubtedly been used by all varieties of wild game, and endlessly succeeding generations of tribesmen. Even now, when it had not been in general use for more than a generation, except for the timeless forest-dust, the old trail was as clear, as solid, as it had ever been.

It also followed a characteristic of nearly all natural trails; nowhere along its full length through the hulking mountains, did it deliberately climb upwards, if there was any other way to surmount an obstacle. It angled here and there, switched back and forth, zig-zagging along steep slopes, and always kept climbing, but by following the route of least endeavor.

Tomahawk was riding a yard or two out front, when Frank called for him to watch for a white-water creek; they would rest up there. The 'breed eased ahead as far as the watercourse, then swung down, loosened the cinch on his saddle, slipped the bridle to water his animal, and turned to face Frank as he said, 'Damned Indians was pretty smart at that.'

Frank and Curtis grinned, and also favored their animals. Afterwards, while allowing the horse to pick feed along the creekbank, Curtis said, 'Tomahawk, why'd you ever leave the reservation and commence working so hard for a living?'

The 'breed looked darkly at his rangeboss. 'What the hell are you talking about, Curtis? I never lived on no reservation. And if you think cowboyin' is hard work, try keeping enough wood around a hide house to keep folks from freezing to death in wintertime. I had an aunt, uncle, and a nest of cousins lived on the Crow reserve, and used to go visit 'em once in a while. You know—even in the fall of the year, the whole blasted family spent all their time hunting firewood. Those damned tipis got a big hole at the top and heat goes out up there faster'n you can throw it into the stone-ring. No sir; them as want that life can sure as hell have my share of it.'

Curtis winked at Frank. 'But you learnt a lot of bad habits from the whites, Tomahawk.'

The 'breed cowboy put a black-eyed stare upon Curtis. 'What are you doing, trying to get a rise out of me? Yeah, I learnt bad habits from the whites—but don't kid yourself, those blanket-people got habits just as bad.' He kept staring steadily at Curtis. 'I'll tell you one thing, Curtis; the more I see and the longer I live, the more I'm convinced don't neither redman nor whiteman have any edge on *either* good or bad. If there's any *real* difference between them, it's that they don't speak the same language. I figure, if they had been able to talk more, they'd have seen how much they are alike. Not that that would have stopped any of the wars, but it would have helped a lot afterwards.'

Tomahawk looked at his horse, then looked up the trail, eyes narrowed as he studied afternoon shadows. 'Frank, we got to stand around here until dark, while I educate Curtis, or do we head on out?'

Frank and Curtis laughed as they moved over to snug up cinches. Even Tomahawk smiled a little.

They went up the crooked, wide trail again, and by now the shadows had circled far around and were beginning to thicken, to firm up, on the right side of the three horsemen, instead of being weaker, and on the left side as they had been a couple of hours before.

The heat was noticeable. More so on the exposed trail than it had been in among the trees. The silence, too, was noticeable. It was only shattered when the three riders passed through some excited blue-jays' private realm, and were scathingly denounced from low tree limbs to the very border of the bird's domain.

Chapter Thirteen

INTO THE SILENT NIGHT

They had roughly an hour of daylight left when Frank, riding a few yards ahead, saw the ancient campsite on up through the trees, and signaled for Tomahawk and Curtis to leave the trail and head over there, up through the trees, which they did, making not a sound once their shod saddle-animals stepped upon the eons-old, spongy pine-needle carpet.

Frank remained out upon the trail, in full sight. Not that he actually expected to have to draw anyone's attention away from his skulking companions; he was confident that old camp had been abandoned early this morning, but being careful rarely resulted in accidental or inadvertent injuries.

He was almost correct. When Tomahawk and Curtis broke out of the final fringe of big trees into the shadowed clearing, there was no one in sight, but to the west of the campsite, out where lush grass grew, a lame sorrel horse whirled and threw up his head.

Frank, turning in from the roadway, saw the man moving through some trees and stepped to the ground, shouldered his carbine and called out.

'Hold it!'

The moving man whirled, saw the aimed Winchester, and leaned to peer more intently, then swore. 'Damn it all, anyway. Why'n hell don't you fellers sing out when you're sneakin' up on folks?'

The man had beard stubble, a crushed old hat atop his awry hair, and an unkempt, unwashed appearance, but he was recognizable to the cowmen once he left the shadows and stood in sunlight. He was the Texan who ran the liverybarn down in Bivouac, a sly-faced, ungrammatical man for whom Frank Kandelin had no particular fondness.

Curtis and Tomahawk rode on up and stepped down. There was abundant evidence that more than one man had camped in this place recently. Bits of greasy paper showed where men had eaten the food they had hastily bundled up to take along before leaving town. There were racks everywhere, as well as wilting pine-needles gathered the previous evening to be placed beneath blanket-rolls.

The Texan pointed out to the lame sorrel and said, 'Wouldn't you know it. I'm the one feller in the country who's got plenty of sound horses, and the one I picked because I figured he'd be stoutest, turned up lame this morning.'

Frank ignored that to ask where the remaining two town-possemen were. The Texan waved his arm in a vague movement. 'Up yonder somewhere. Them, and some fellers who come up yesterday to he'p; fellers from old Underwood's cow outfit. They taken to the trail early, right after breakfast, and I haven't heard nothing since they pulled out.' The liveryman warmed to his topic. 'Them outlaws come in this far, overland, from the southeast. They must have had one hell of a hard ride of it, because that's bad country down there. That's where my horse first commenced to favor.'

'Did the outlaws find the trail?' Frank asked, and the Texan vigorously bobbed his head.

'Yeah. We could read their sign before we bedded down last night. They found it, all right, and they was long gone by sundown, so we turned in, figuring to make up time today.'

Tomahawk looked disgustedly at the sharp-featured liveryman, and drifted his disgruntled gaze on around to Frank. He said, 'Let's get out of here,' and waited for Frank to agree.

It was Curtis who asked a direct question about the fugitives. 'What did the outlaws leave behind, besides their tracks?'

The Texan pointed. 'Empty tins of beef and peaches, and that rag with blood on it.'

Tomahawk's expression underwent a swift change. He walked over, retrieved the soiled rag and returned to the others, while he examined it. With a grunt he passed it to Curtis. 'Looks like they didn't get clean away,' he opined, and Curtis agreed, then handed the rag to Frank.

The blood was dark and it had dried swiftly, but the injury it had come from could have been relatively minor. The Texan seemed to believe this was the case, because as Frank examined the rag, he said, 'We talked about that, last night. I wasn't up near the bank when they busted out of there on the run, but the other two fellers was, and they said three of those fellers was about clear of the north end of town before the firing started.' He shrugged. 'It could be someone made a lucky hit, but more'n likely this hurt feller got his injury somewhere on the trail—maybe from a low tree-limb.'

Frank tossed the rag down and nodded at Tomahawk, who was showing his impatience again. They got back into the saddle and left the Texan looking after them as they headed out to the trail, and north-ward again.

The day was nearly spent. If this had been a month or two hence, they could have counted upon a couple more hours of daylight, even in the mountains. As it was, the gloom began to descend, gradually but with a darker substance to it where the forests on each side of the wide trail stood tallest, and by the time they were a mile or more beyond the campsite, dusk was well on its way.

Frank was in the lead again, and did not halt until he had two twin spires in sight about a mile ahead. That was where they had to go through the one good ambushing-place on the entire trail. They discussed this, decided that both the outlaws and the possemen had long since passed through and beyond, and rode ahead. But Tomahawk was uneasy until they got to the far side, where the ridge flattened somewhat, and the nearest high upthrusts were several hundred yards distant, on each side.

Curtis had his sack of tobacco to take the edges off his pangs of hunger, and Tomahawk yanked some tubers from the ground in a grassy place, and chewed on them. He offered a handful to Frank, but got back a wry grin and a head-shake. 'My trouble is, I got civilized innards,' he told the cowboy, and Tomahawk rode along chewing as though an unpleasant after-effect were inconceivable to him.

On the far side of the pass they would normally have had good visibility, except that as the gloom deeply descended, the best they could manage was a clear sighting on ahead for a couple of hundred yards, and even that visibility began to fill up with darkness after they had been traveling another hour and a half.

Frank halted occasionally to listen, which was the only one of their five senses which was as good in darkness as in daylight. But they were able to hear nothing at all.

There would be a moon, but during the long interim after sundown and before moon-rise, they rode along, not in any haste, listened as often as Frank thought it advisable, and waited for moon-rise.

Once, they were slammed back against the cantles and jarred wide awake when a startled black bear shambling along whining and grumbling to himself, stepped out upon the trail two dozen yards ahead, and their horses almost panicked.

So did the bear, who had expected nothing like three mounted men to be athwart his path. He whirled and fled with surprising speed for such a loosely-

120

connected, ungainly-looking creature. By the time the riders had their terrified mounts back under control, and Tomahawk had his sixgun out, mad as a hornet, the black bear had disappeared into the black night on the east side of the old trail.

Tomahawk cursed with heartfelt feeling, slammed his gun back into its holster, and bleakly rode along with one gimlet eye cocked ahead for another such encounter, but there was none, and there wouldn't have been this time either, if that hadn't been an old gummer-bear, too slowed by age and too fuddled in the head to be wary.

They crossed flat country upon the rims, which was not unusual in genuine mountains. About the only place a top-out broke sharply was where the landforms rose abruptly and broke away abruptly. This country had a broad, plateau-like summit. There was good grass up here, and hoary old pines and firs, along with a few white oaks. It would have been an ideal place to run cattle except for two things; there were predators all around, and the second reason was harder to correct; cattle would not climb this high, unless horsemen pushed them, and as soon as the horsemen turned back, so would the cattle.

They crossed good-grass country for a solid hour, then Tomahawk called softly for Frank to halt. He pointed down the far slope where a thin beam of light seemed to rise up from the east of the trail in among the spiky black silhouettes of giant trees.

If it was a campfire, it was not just distant, it was

121

also farther to the east than it seemed likely either the outlaws or their pursuers would travel. On the other hand, if it *was* a campfire, it almost had to be one party or the other.

They rode slowly to the far edge, where the trail tipped downward again, northward, and stopped another hour farther along, because as they continued to descend, treetops would effectively hide that weak light. They confirmed that it *was* a campfire, and as they resumed their riding, they discussed whether to head over and scout it up, which would cost them precious time, or whether to assume it was a hunting party—or maybe even other renegades, for all they knew—and keep steadily on the trail.

Tomahawk finally resolved things by volunteering to make a big sashay through the dark forest and see who was out there, and if it was the possemen, to head back for a rendezvous with Frank and Curtis, who would be riding slowly. On the other hand, if Tomahawk thought those men were the outlaws, he was to hasten back and give the alarm.

They passed down-country for another hour, then Tomahawk wordlessly turned off into the trees. No one thought about his chances of missing the camp altogether in all those dark miles of unfamiliar forest.

Curtis rolled another smoke when his stomach began to rumble. Frank, who had been through here before, described the view of the north country, which they could not see in the darkness. Moab, he told Curtis, was east of them, and northward, over where the stageroad ran, perhaps as much as fifty or sixty miles. He shook his head. 'Why those damned fools didn't head on up there, I'll never know. All they had to do was keep parallel to the road.'

'Except that they'd know damned well posses would be boiling out all over the countryside, looking for them, and the first thing most fellers would figure, would be that they'd do just exactly that.'

Frank was implacable. 'This way, they're goners. They can't even steal fresh horses until they get out on the grassland again, and by then we'll be too close.'

Curtis blew smoke, eyed the high vault of heaven with its interminable expanse of twinkling blue-white stars, and sighed aloud as he dropped his head to the onward trail. However this ended for him, for *all* of them including the possemen and the outlaws, it was going to be a hell of a long ride back.

For those able to ride back.

The moon came, finally, a foot at a time, cold-looking and with one corner worn away somewhat. It was in no hurry to make its time-hallowed high crossing, and for a while it seemed to be balancing upon a distant ridge. Then it lurched higher, cleared the ridge and began its ponderous climb. The light improved almost at once. Frank and Curtis were able to see the plains miles onward, but they looked like something out of an eerie dream, their forms made flat, without appreciable depth or height, and their vast expanse as obscure as a view from beneath the sea, looking upwards.

But any increase in visibility was welcome, because it allowed Frank to swing off and walk ahead of his horse, detecting an occasional sign made by shod hooves. When he was satisfied with what he had seen, he said, 'If that's the outlaws Tomahawk went over to scout up, they must have cut inland from down near the flat country, which means we're still a long distance behind them.'

Curtis had no comment to make about that. He studied the location of the rising moon, and made a guess about the time. 'Got to be a little after midnight, Frank.'

He was correct, and as the night-chill settled in, they had additional reason to believe he was correct.

They had the flattening-out, narrowing far end of the downhill trail in sight when Frank halted. They both dismounted down here, willing to waste a little time in the hope that Tomahawk would overtake them.

If he was coming, and no matter how soft the forest-footing was in among the trees, the night was so totally silent now that they would pick up his sounds without difficulty.

Frank turned up his collar, buttoned his coat, and wished ruefully he'd brought along his riding-coat, which was lined with blanketing material. The suit-coat he was wearing—a concession to Ella and the funeral he had expected to attend—was nice enough looking, but was just barely better than no covering at all, when it came to keeping the cold out.

Chapter Fourteen

THE SIGHTING!

Coyotes, coursing along the lower-down country, probably following musky deer-scent which would be strong throughout the browse-country of the lower foothills, came like shaggy grey ghosts across the trail a few yards northward, and saw the men before the men saw them. The coyotes did not wait for a confirming second look, they exploded in all directions, several yipping—probably pups, because older coyotes would not waste a single breath—streaking away in a belly-down run.

Frank watched and did nothing. Another time he would have been able to account for at least two, and perhaps three or four, of the fleeing pack. Tonight, one gunshot would be the same as announcing their presence at a time when they preferred not to be expected.

Curtis, standing near the head of his horse, felt a slight tug, and turned. The horse had his head raised, ears pointing towards the forest. Curtis grunted and pointed. Frank turned to also look and listen.

The horses caught a scent long before the men heard a sound, but eventually they picked up something that could be a man proceeding through the trees southward of them. Or it could be another fuddleheaded old gummer-bear reduced to nocturnal hunting because, by broad daylight, he was neither clever enough, nor fast enough any longer, to be a daylight hunter.

But it wasn't a bear, otherwise the horses would not have reacted by simply standing and staring. Frank handed Curtis his reins, drew his sixgun and walked silently over into the first tier of trees, then moved down the trail towards the place in the middle-distance where the oncoming visitor would leave the forest and touch the trail.

Frank heard the sound he had been waiting for: Spur-rowels making their tiny music as a man's booted feet brushed through underbrush. He raised the sixgun, thumb upon the hammer, waited until he finally had the rider in sight, then slowly lowered the weapon and said, 'You made pretty damned good time,' as Tomahawk emerged into the moonlight upon the trail.

Tomahawk was surprised. 'Hell; I never figured we'd be this close, when I got back over here.' He swung down and walked with his horse back up to where Curtis was standing. Then he looked at his companions, and groaned aloud. 'You'd never guess what that is, out yonder. Four Bible-bangers with an old canvas-topped wagon, sitting around a little supper fire takin' turns reading from the Good Book to each other.' Tomahawk turned to look at his horse, pityingly. 'Damned shame to use up strength on *that* sort of a scout.' He turned back. 'Mormons,' he announced. 'No one else in his right mind would be 'way out here, where there's no town and no houses that I ever seen, poking around.'

Frank asked if the 'breed had spoken to the people, and for the first time, Tomahawk did not look disgruntled. He smiled. 'Yeah. I figured I had a drink coming, or at least a little fun, so I tied the horse back in the trees, stuffed my hat inside my coat, jumped out into their firelight and waved my pistol around . . . If you ever seen praying folks stop praying and commence sweating even on a cold night, it was them. They had a bottle of whiskey—for snake-bite, naturally. I sat and drank and told them about this big band of bloody-hand killers and renegades ranging all through the hills, and us fellers trying to find them, and I'll tell you—you never saw folks get off their backsides so fast and commence chucking camp-gear into an old wagon.'

'Did they see riders?' demanded Curtis, and Tomahawk shook his head. 'Nope. Haven't seen any horsemen since they left some place called Beaverton, northeast of us a few hundert miles.' Tomahawk reached inside his coat and triumphantly held forth a whiskey bottle which was three-quarters full. 'Didn't make the whole damned ride for nothing,' he announced, and passed the bottle around.

They all drank, then mounted up as the chill turned into a genuine cold frost, and headed on down across the lower foothills out towards the yonder plain where moonlight had made a few changes, as its source had risen high enough to be almost directly above them.

The whiskey was not the substitute for a blanket-coat Frank would have voluntarily chosen, but it was certainly better than no alternative at all, and for Curtis, whose empty stomach had begun to rebel against tobacco, the whiskey did not so much fill a need as it filled a very necessary requirement: Additional body heat. As long as the whiskey lasted, or if sunshine-warmth came again, first, Curtis would be just fine, but eventually the whiskey was not going to be able to satisfy the need for genuine warmth.

Frank guessed it had to be close to four or five o'clock in the morning, by the time they came out through the last thin stand of trees, and here, the trail fanned out, as though its most prominent users, recently, wild game of all kinds, went different ways in search of different needs.

Frank suddenly halted. This time there was no question about it being a campfire. There were no trees to hinder visibility, and it was the only far brilliance upon that entire, enormous plain of grassland.

They sat and gazed far out through a period of long silence, then Tomahawk turned stiffly to study the eastern sky, before saying, 'That looks like it's a hell of a long way off, and the way I figure it, we're only about an hour off from first-light.' He turned. 'If we can't get up close to those fellers, when dawn comes, they're sure as hell going to see us riding towards them.'

It was a sound statement and Frank nodded his

head about it while he continued to study the distant fire. 'They're already getting ready to strike camp,' he told Tomahawk and Curtis. 'Otherwise, no one would have pitched a handful of wood on their fire.'

Curtis took no part in this discussion. When the others rode out again, he went along, still silent, and still interested in just how close they might be able to get, before daylight caught them out in the middle of the vast plain, in clear sight of anyone who cared to look at them.

Frank shrank from doing it, but as soon as they were well clear of the foothills, he booted his mount over into a steady lope and held him at it for almost a full hour. At this steady gait, they covered miles of open country, and encountered one deep arroyo, the only break in the flatness over which they rode. Then they hauled down to a walk.

There was a thin, pale streak of watery light inches above the eastern horizon, dividing the darkness above from the earth below. Tomahawk had guessed things correctly. They were still out in the middle of nowhere, and that fire which looked fading and weaker now, did not seem to be very much closer to them.

One of the exasperations associated with great distances and clear air, was that a man could ride towards a particular viewable point of reference all day long, and find it no closer at sunset than it had been at sunrise. This was how Frank viewed that distant fire. Of course it *was* closer, but it did not *seem* to be any closer at all, and what was most troubling of all, was that the inches-wide blue strip of light between heaven and earth, was becoming steadily wider as the time passed. False dawn was only a short while away, and after that—daylight.

Frank could not push the horses more than he already had. It was a minor miracle that they had held up as well as they had; if they had not been the results of selective ranch-breeding and good care, they wouldn't have, either.

He twisted in the saddle to look at his companions, and Curtis finally spoke. 'We're going to be seen, one way or another, Frank. Even if we ran the horses—and they didn't collapse under us—we still couldn't get up there before they are going to spot us. So—if we split off; Tomahawk heading easterly, far out beyond sight, then on around, me to the west, doing the same thing, and you poking along so's they'll see you and keep watching you—*maybe* we can catch them.'

Tomahawk was willing, because he nodded approval, but as he kept his black gaze riveted upon the paling-out distant fire, he also had something to say. 'And suppose that's the posse, and not the out-laws?' He looked past at Frank. 'We'll have used up more horse-flesh for nothing.'

If there was a third way, Frank could not find it, so he acted on what Curtis had said. 'Head on out, Tom-ahawk—and if *you* can see *them* when they strike camp, remember, they'll also be able to see you. Make it the biggest surround of your life, and when you meet Curtis, ride back down towards the camp.' He considered the fire for a moment, then blew out a tired breath. 'If it's the renegades, then we had to have ridden right past the possemen in the darkness—and that doesn't seem likely to me. They'd have heard us, sure.'

Tomahawk demurred. 'Not if they was off the trail a half mile or more—which is where I'd have gone if I was in their boots—because I wouldn't want my throat cut in my blankets.'

Frank gestured, Tomahawk turned eastward, Curtis turned westerly, and Frank fished around inside his coat for his tobacco and papers, rolled a smoke, lit it, and crushed it out atop the saddlehorn almost immediately because the taste was terrible.

As long as he could see Tomahawk and Curtis, he worried, but the light of false-dawn did not really arrive until Tomahawk, who was riding in that direction—eastward—was no longer visible, so in the end he had been worrying for no good reason.

The fire was either dying, or dawn was making it harder to see, by the time Frank got several additional miles onward, but there was a thin, straight-standing rope of soiled smoke rising upwards, which had not been visible in the darkness, and he set his course according to that.

When he was close enough to see horses and smaller figures, false-dawn had passed and the first smoke-blue shafts had begun to turn softly pink. He saw one of the smaller figures walk forward a short distance, away from the camp facing up in Frank's direction. He also saw this small figure hang a carbine in the crook of one arm as he watched Frank.

The clue as to which party he was approaching lay in the number of men at the camp, and he swore because the light was not good enough yet, and the moving horses further inhibited his head-counting, as he made a rough estimate about the distance, intending to halt just beyond carbine-range.

The sun inched upwards, pink light turned to a sharper, deflected brilliance, and light-columns shot upwards in the direction of the sky.

Frank halted and stepped off his horse, yanked loose his carbine and stood hip-shot, watching the men who were also watching him. More daylight came, and this time it flooded downward and outward, filling the night-chilled vast plain with adequate light.

There were three men and three horses up at that camp! He had overtaken the outlaws! It was anyone's guess where the possemen were, and right at this moment Frank did not speculate about that.

While two of the distant men resumed their work at saddling the horses, the third man, still in place with the Winchester slung across one arm, kept his vigil. He and Frank faced one another across a distance both could clearly see over, now that another day was at hand, but which neither could effectively fire across.

Frank relaxed. He was tired and hungry and cold, but momentarily none of these things seemed worth considering. The temporary body-heat provided by whiskey had died out, leaving Frank more wrung out than if he had drunk no whiskey at all. Nevertheless he smiled a little. As long as those outlaws were watching *him*, Tomahawk and Curtis were completing their surround to get in behind the outlaws, to commence riding down-country towards them. Whatever happened next, the outlaws were in for a surprise.

One of the outlaws walked over and thrust a pair of reins into the free hand of the sentinel, who now stood with his horse at his back. The animal looked dispirited, even after a night-long rest and hours of grazing, and even at that distance. Frank was a lifelong horseman, he knew the stance of a worn-out saddlehorse when he saw one even across hundreds of yards of a cold, sunlit late springtime morning.

The horses he and his friends were riding were also ridden down, but not *that* badly. If this encounter turned into a running fight, the outlaws were not going to win that, either.

Frank considered yelling down to the outlaws, identifying himself and calling for their surrender. The reason he did not do it was because, while he was thinking about it, all three outlaws climbed across leather and turned northward, leaving their smoking, dying fire behind in the dazzling newday sunlight.

They were riding straight into Curtis and Tomahawk.

Chapter Fifteen

THE MEETING

Frank was in no hurry. He allowed the outlaws to cover a hundred yards before mounting and riding in their wake. He tried to guess which one of them had been injured, but at this distance it was impossible to tell, except that all the outlaws rode wearily, but none more slouched than the others.

Evidently the man who had shed that bandage back on the far side of the mountains was not very critically injured, or he would be distinguishable from his companions.

Frank twisted a couple of times to gaze back in the direction of the foothills. He half-believed Tomahawk's theory about the possemen having bedded down somewhere off the trail, back there in the trees. But there was no sign of other horsemen.

He did eventually catch sight of a different kind of movement, however. This sighting occurred when they were all a mile farther overland.

It was a baggy-topped old covered wagon heading away from the forest northward, upcountry parallel with the horsemen, but far behind them. That would be the Mormons Tomahawk had encountered last night, and frightened half out of their wits. They were

134

probably heading away from the forest in order to have a clear view on all sides as they fled the area where Tomahawk had told them a band of outlaws was marauding.

The outlaws also saw that old wagon. Frank saw them draw rein and stare, then they pushed onward again, only occasionally looking back to be certain Frank was still behind them.

He began worrying about Curtis and Tomahawk, believing he should have seen them by now, even though it was an immense expanse of open, grassland-country on ahead, conceivably veined with run-off arroyos like the deep one he had encountered hours earlier, and which were not visible until a rider was almost upon the verge of one of them.

Finally, as he twisted to look back, he saw riders coming swiftly from the direction of the distant foothills, and counted them. It looked like six men, and by his best estimate the posse consisted of either five or six men. Also, having obviously seen Frank, and the three outlaws ahead of Frank, they were hurrying to effect a juncture.

As he watched, the possemen split up, half riding easterly, the remaining half heading out westerly. Both groups, though, were also making a big, sweeping curve, apparently to do exactly as Curtis and Tomahawk had done—get around the outlaws while remaining beyond gun-range, to cut them off.

Frank straightened in the saddle, anxiously. It

would not take the renegades long to guess what was in progress.

The sun was above the horizon now, heat was coming into the fresh, new morning to winnow away the stiffness in both Frank and his horse. By mid-day it was going to be hot out upon the big plain.

Someone, a long distance off, fired a sixgun. The roar was muted by the time it reached Frank, but it was the unmistakable, deep-down bellow of a .45; carbines did not make that kind of a sound.

Frank tugged his hat brim in low and scanned the onward country without seeing anything which resembled mounted men. The outlaws halted. They too were scanning the onward range. Like Frank, they were sure that gunshot had come from up ahead, somewhere.

Frank drew rein and sat watching the outlaws. They could see the old wagon behind them, to the east. They always had Frank in sight, dogging their tracks like a wily wolf, and those swiftly hurrying, fanned-out possemen were also in sight by now. But all these pursuers were *behind* them; a considerable distance behind them in fact. But that solitary gunshot had *not* been behind them, and while they could no more see anyone up ahead than Frank had been able to, obviously someone had to be out there, and this thought appeared to be holding the outlaws immobile.

Frank's anxiety kept mounting. He was aware of something the bank-robbers had not yet comprehended, in their fixed concentration on the country lying ahead: Those hard-riding, very distant possemen were sweeping constantly closer in their far-flung surround. While the renegades sat there, trying to evolve a course of action, the possemen were closing their big trap.

Finally, the outlaws hauled out their carbines and resumed their way northward. Frank caught sight of reflected sunlight off grey steel, and shook his head. The outlaws were going to fight, if they could not otherwise break clear, and in Frank's opinion, this kind of open country was a poor place to be, with someone aiming at you.

Eventually, the renegades comprehended what those hurrying horsemen were trying to do. They halted again, this time gesturing as they talked. Frank tried to guess their reaction, but when they turned back in his direction, peering along their back-trail in the direction of the far-away forests, he could not believe they would try to flee in that direction. They would be heading back towards the territory where by now cowmen would be swarming over the range in search of them.

One outlaw dismounted, facing Frank, handed his reins to another outlaw, then walked back in Frank's direction very deliberately, Winchester in the crook of his arm.

It looked to Frank like the same man who had watched him before; at least he held his saddlegun in the same manner.

Then the man stopped, studied Frank who was sitting motionless upon his horse, and finally dropped to one knee. Frank did not wait for the man to hoist his carbine, he whirled and loped his horse back a hundred yards, then faced northward again.

The kneeling man was now standing, Winchester grounded, staring at Frank, who was again far beyond carbine-range. While they stared at one another, the outlaw called back and a companion brought up his saddle-animal. The outlaw mounted it and still faced Frank, carbine across his saddle-swells.

The heat was pleasant, the morning was advancing—and now, finally, those possemen had the outlaws cut off from three sides, northward, easterly and westerly. They were strung out, watching and waiting. Only when Frank took his eyes off the man who had wanted to try a long shot at him, did he notice that there were more than five men, strung out barring the outlaws' upcountry flight. There were seven men, and while he could not be certain at that distance, he was confident two of them had to be Curtis and Tomahawk.

A number of things had changed, since sunup. The most important one, to Frank Kandelin, was the fact that he, and only he, now barred the retreat of those renegades back towards the mountains and the forest, lying southward. The same forest and mountains they had all traversed the preceding night.

It was a lonely feeling. He looked out where the old wagon with its soiled canvas covering was crawling steadily along, almost parallel with the surrounded outlaws by now, its driver seeming to be totally blind to what was so dramatically taking place a couple of miles west of him. The wagon pushed steadily northward without deviating a foot in any direction.

The outlaws had another of those mounted conferences, then abruptly turned back towards Frank, riding slowly. Their decision, evidently, was to try and regain the protection of the southward mountains. It had to be a forlorn, last hope for them, at least Frank saw it in that light, as he checked his carbine and yanked loose the tie-down on his Colt, and rested his horse while watching the advancing renegades.

Far back—so distant, in fact, they looked no larger than ants—the possemen began closing their line and walking towards the withdrawing renegades. Frank sighed; it would have helped if those men had made some attempt to get out and around the outlaws, and closer to Frank.

He kept close watch on the intervening distance, eventually dismounted, stepped ahead of his horse trailing one split-rein, and knelt, Winchester in hand. This stopped the outlaws again. They may have expected Frank to retreat, as they came towards him, and when he instead showed fight, they had to consider the possibilities.

He shouldered the saddlegun, picked a target, pulled the man down the barrel to him, then, just before squeezing the trigger, he elevated the barrel's stubby tip three inches above the man's hat, and fired.

This time, the explosion was higher and sharper,

and was almost instantly swallowed up in the immensity of the prairie silence.

He lowered the gun, waited, and when the man flinched, Frank levered up his next round, and waited. His slug had come close. Maybe if he did not elevate quite so high, next time. He raised the carbine again, sighted with infinite care, but before he could fire, that foremost outlaw suddenly hooked his horse. The startled animal gave a big bound and lit down racing directly at Frank, his rider curled low down alongside the animal's neck, the man's carbine extended, one-handed, as he made his charge.

Frank stood up quickly, jerked his horse sideways and moved away just as the outlaw fired. He did not even see where the slug struck, but firing one-handedly from the plunging back of a racing horse was not conducive to marksmanship in any case.

The outlaw jerked his Winchester upwards, then violently downwards, the lever dropped, then jerked upwards, re-charging the weapon. No one but an experienced Winchester-man could have done that so well.

Frank sprang across leather hauling his horse to the east. The astonished animal responded with a snort, and plunged sidewards as the second gunshot sounded. This time Frank thought he saw dust spurt behind him, but he spent no more than a second looking back. He raised his own Winchester with both hands and fired, then dropped the saddlegun and drew his Colt as he spurred the agitated animal beneath him, and made a zig-zagging run off to one side of the oncoming renegade.

They were going to pass one another, one racing southward, one racing northward, at a distance of roughly a hundred and fifty yards. Frank leaned down the off-side of his animal, snapped off a pistol-shot, then straightened slightly in the saddle as the outlaw clawed at his mount's whipping mane, jerking his horse in a yawning, slamming change of gait to veer away from Frank. The man flung aside his carbine. Frank saw his right hand going for the hip-holstered Colt, and fired twice more, fast.

The next moment the racing horse was running free, head and tail high, the saddle empty.

Frank straightened up looking back. The outlaw was on the ground, rolling. Frank slammed his horse into a sliding, dirt-spewing halt, then turned him and loped back towards the fallen man, cocked Colt up and ready.

Someone in the distance let go with a keening high wail, but Frank did not take his eyes off the man in the grass until he was no more than two hundred feet away.

The outlaw was lying on his stomach, arms out-flung. He still had the sixgun gripped in his right fist.

Frank swung his horse sidewards and called to the renegade. 'Let go of the gun!'

The man did not move, so Frank risked a rearward glance, and saw the other two outlaws heading straight for him, carbines in hand, and made a swift decision. He sprang from the saddle and rushed forward. The man in the grass raised his head, rolled his body sideways, and clumsily threw up his gun-hand, but Frank was too close; he aimed a savage kick, caught the man's arm, and the gun flew out of the prone man's hand. The force of the kick rolled the prone man completely over, and this time he did not attempt to raise up again, but lay flat out in the grass on his back.

Frank whirled, pulled the horse to him, vaulted up across leather and hooked the beast before his feet were in the stirrups, running diagonally across the front of the oncoming renegades. They both fired at him, and both missed, but one slug must have come close enough to inspire his mount, because the animal suddenly found a fresh source of energy, and broke ahead in a flinging, belly-down run, which carried Frank out of gun-range in moments.

He fought the excited animal down to a halt, and turned to look back. Neither of those fleeing men so much as looked over in the direction of their fallen companion. They raced away southward, in the direction of the distant mountains.

Coming in their wake, grimly silent and riding hard, were Curtis, Tomahawk, and those possemen, and as Frank watched, the possemen began to close the distance.

The outlaws on their spent horses could not possibly get all the way back to the forest.

Chapter Sixteen

ANOTHER MOONLIT NIGHT

For Frank, the fight was over. He walked his winded horse back, retrieved his Winchester, booted it, then led the horse behind him as he walked out where the prone man still lay on his back, unmoving.

The wagonload of Mormon missionaries, or whatever they were, was still boring steadily northward, absolutely blind to everything which was taking place a couple of miles west and southward of them. Undoubtedly they had witnessed the strange horseback duel between Frank and the fallen renegade, but they neither changed course nor altered the gait of their team; they kept rolling northward.

This far south in Utah, and even over the territorial line into Arizona, was Mormon country. Not as strongly as elsewhere in Utah, perhaps, but it was still Mormon country. Whatever those people in the wagon were up to, proselyting or on a 'mission', or just plain caravanning to the Glory of God and his angel Moroni, this was the country for them to be doing it in, and if they chose not to become involved in the fight west of them, that was their business.

Frank hardly more than glanced after them as he walked over and stood looking at the man in the grass.

The man looked straight back. He did not move, but he seemed to be entirely capable of movement; at least his stare upwards at Frank was totally rational.

The outlaw's sixgun lay shinily in the grass several yards distant, but the man had made no move to retrieve it, and as Frank stood above him, now, the outlaw said, 'You got any whiskey?'

Frank shook his head.

The renegade was a dark-skinned, grey-eyed, dissipated, hard-faced individual, in his forties, greying, thickly, muscularly built, and covered now with beard-stubble, dirt, and stale sweat. He said, 'Where's my horse?'

Frank raised his eyes scanning the sunbright plain. There was no sign of the horse, but in the southward distance the two remaining, fleeing outlaws were in sight, and almost close enough to use their carbines, were their pursuers. Frank looked down as he said, 'I don't see him. But you're not going anywhere.'

There was blood on the lower part of the man's body, on the right side. Frank's bullet must have barely cleared the top of the saddlehorn to strike the outlaw that low. While the man had been lying stomach-down, the wound had not been visible. Now it was.

The outlaw sighed. 'Put my hat over my eyes,' he said.

Frank went after the hat and placed it to shield the outlaw's eyes from hot sunlight. The man said, 'Thanks. Who'n hell are you, anyway? Lawman?'

'Cowman,' replied Frank. 'I had three thousand dollars in the Bivouac bank.' He stepped around to where his horse and himself would provide more shade for the wounded man. 'Mike Leland is dead,' he announced, and the outlaw squinted upwards from beneath his hat brim.

'We figured that,' he replied, his voice more tired-sounding than weak-sounding. 'What happened to him?'

'Tied his reins instead of looping them, out front of the bank, and couldn't jerk them loose before half the town opened up on him.'

The outlaw sighed. 'He never had it in him. Best shot amongst us, but he never had it in him, in other ways . . . He had a wife and kid.'

Frank looked down-country, but now the fleeing outlaws and the pursuing possemen were barely discernible. It sounded as though there were gunshots, down there, too, but Frank was not sure. Nor, for the moment, was he particularly concerned. Those remaining two outlaws did not have a chance.

The outlaw spoke again. 'You was plain lucky. Otherwise I'd have nailed you and opened the back-trail for us.'

Frank sighed. 'Maybe, but I doubt it. Not on spent horses, mister.' He studied the bleeding wound a moment. 'What's your name?'

'Carl Holt. We was all miners—only the gold played out.'

'So you took to robbing banks and stages.'

145

The outlaw said, 'What would you have done?'

'Got a job somewhere. On a ranch or in a town.'

Carl Holt's lips pulled downward scornfully. 'Like hell. That don't pay a man a living wage, not out here.'

Frank knelt and rolled a smoke, then offered it to the wounded man, but Holt declined. He did not smoke. But he wistfully mentioned whiskey again, so evidently he drank. Then, looking steadily at Frank, he said, 'How bad's that hole in my guts?'

Frank was honest. 'Bad enough, Carl.'

The outlaw kept gazing at Frank. 'Well; I came from Kansas. But there's no one back there, so you might as well plant me right here.' He closed his eyes, then sprang them open again. 'Your three thousand dollars is in the saddlebags on my horse.' He closed his eyes again, and this time he did not open them again.

Frank smoked the cigarette, dwarfed to ant-size by the huge expanse of country he was in the center of, the sun rode high across a flawless, turquoise sky, the old Mormon-wagon was small, now, in the heat-blurred distance, and very gradually, Frank could make out riders coming back in his direction from the south. They were bunched up so he could not tell how many there were, but when two broke clear and loped ahead in his direction, he was relieved; whatever had happened down there, at least Curtis and Tomahawk had survived it.

He killed the cigarette in the grass and waited.

Curtis arrived a yard ahead of Tomahawk. They swung off, staring at the dead man in the grass, then Tomahawk said, 'I wanted a look at this one. I never seen that done before, but my paw used to tell me that's how the Crows and the Cheyennes used to duel—on horseback, charging straight at one another. I figured this one might have been a redskin.'

Curtis was less concerned with the duel and the dead man. 'We got the other two. One's wounded—in the rump, of all places—and we picked up this feller's horse running along behind us. The saddlebags—'

'Are stuffed with money,' state Frank, breaking in to make his announcement. 'Where were those damned possemen, last night?'

Tomahawk answered, dryly. 'Right where I figured they was—resting off the trail, back in the trees a mile or so. We rode right past them. But when they come back onto the trail this morning and seen our tracks, they come ahead in a hurry.'

Frank glanced down. 'It's a long ride back,' he said, thinking in terms of a corpse making that rough trip lashed belly-down across his saddle.

Tomahawk looked down, too, then said, 'It won't bother this one as much as it's going to bother that other one who got shot in the pants.'

The posse walked on up, each man looking at the corpse in the grass. Frank knew them all, but one particular man, shaggy-haired and with bristly, reddish whiskers, who was Hal Underwood's rangeboss, Frank knew best. He nodded and the rangeboss nodded back, then smiled at Frank. 'I never saw a gunfight from horseback before,' he said, and, having got that out of his system, he pointed to a tucked-up big sorrel horse. 'Got saddlebags chock full of money. He belonged to this dead feller.'

In the rear of the grimy-looking possemen, were a pair of total strangers. One of them was sitting sideways in his saddle. Frank gazed at them, but his interest in the pair of surviving outlaws was minimal. He was thinking instead of the ride back, so he gestured for someone to lead up the sorrel, while he called upon Curtis and Tomahawk to help boost the dead weight up across leather.

The sun was hot and slightly past its high meridian before they got the corpse lashed into place and were ready to undertake the return trip. No one had a canteen either, but they reached the foothills and a little creek before thirst became much of a discomfort, and they also rested part way up the trail, after tanking up at the creek, so, by the time they had the top-out in sight again, they were not in as bad shape as they could have been in.

Frank and Underwood's rangebosses rode ahead, talking a little, now and then. Tomahawk rode back with the pair of captured bank-robbers, both of whom were rough, profane, hard men, former miners who had turned outlaw exactly as the dead man and Mike Leland had done. The wounded man rode part of the way standing in his stirrups and part of the way cocked sidewards on his saddle-seat. Actually, his wound, aside from being bizarre, especially on a man who had been sitting down when he had been struck, was not as bad as it sounded.

Someone's carbine-bullet had struck the man's five-inch cantle from behind, and most of the bullet's force had been spent, because of the distance, even before it struck the cantle, but nevertheless the pellet had penetrated the cantle, on a downward angle, and had hit the outlaw in the ham, making a big bruise, and a much smaller puncture. The wound had bled considerably, and the outlaw was in discomfort all during the ride back to Bivouac, but the hole in his rump was actually little more than a bad flesh-wound.

He did not get much sympathy, even from his companion, the other outlaw, but he *did* get some sly chiding, mostly from Tomahawk, who thought this had to be the most unique, and funny, gun-wound he had ever heard of. By the time they reached the top-out and were heading across to the far, Bivouac, side of the mountain, the injured outlaw had formed a violent dislike for Tomahawk.

They could have halted at early dusk, or even before, during the hot, long late afternoon. They, and their animals, were certainly very much in need of a long rest, but Frank wanted to get back, so they kept riding.

The heat favored them; it did not diminish even when they were well along on the south slope where giant trees pretty well filtered out late sunlight, even before evening arrived. It also made them lethargic, but all any of them had to do was look back, where the dead outlaw was flopping feelinglessly along, to be brought back to full wakefulness. It was one of those sights that unnerved even tough, strong men.

The horses plodded, and occasionally stumbled. Ordinarily, rangemen yanked up a stumbling horse. Not this time; the chase had been harder on the animals, even than it had been on their riders.

Finally, when the moon arrived, with a little more worn away from one side than had shown up as being worn off the previous night, they were well down the mountain, with the warmth beginning to finally leave.

Underwood's russet-stubbled rangeboss dozed in the saddle from time to time, and only remained fully awake when Frank mentioned what was uppermost in his mind, now that the bank-robbers had been apprehended, and the money recovered: Ella.

The rangeboss had not known that Leland had a wife, nor had he known that she was staying at the Kandelin cow-outfit, and those things were enough to jar him fully awake. He eyed Frank quizzically and asked questions which Frank answered shortly. Then the rangeboss scratched his jaw, peered outward and downward, far ahead where it was just barely possible to discern town-lights, and said, 'What kind of a damnfool turns to bank-robbery when he's got a family?'

The cowboy seemed unable to co-relate those two things, as though the renegade's trade were something only single men ever engaged in. But, he was right, so Frank answered him.

'You just named it—a damn fool. But he's dead and buried, so that lets him out of it. I'm thinking about her and the two little boys.'

The rangeboss, a single man, had nothing to offer on this, so he rode along pondering the uniqueness of Frank's revelation, and did not doze off again, not even when they reached the low foothills and Frank reined up to say, 'From here on, they're all yours.' The rangeboss was entirely agreeable. To reach his home-ranch he had to go within a mile of town anyway.

Curtis leaned and pulled loose the saddlebags from behind the dead man's saddle, slung them over his shoulder, and when the riders split off, he headed for FK with more money on his back than he had ever seen, all at one time, in his entire life. But he was too tired to make any comment about this, and even tough, rugged Tomahawk, ignored the saddle-bags and concentrated on looking for a lighted bunkhouse on ahead through the moonlit, silent long night.

Chapter Seventeen

THE RETURN

It was very late when they entered the yard, but there was a light up at the mainhouse, and also one down at the bunkhouse. In fact, Slim must have been listening for them, because they had scarcely got over in front of the barn before he came hurrying forth from the bunkhouse, full of questions which no one really felt much like answering.

Frank handed the reins of his horse to Slim with instructions to see that all the horses were grained, then hayed, and turned into a corral—not stalls. Curtis handed over the saddlebags, and Frank struck out for the mainhouse lugging the saddlebags with him, trailing them in the dust as though they did not contain anything of value.

Ella was sewing in the parlor. She had a fire on the hearth, and to help pass the time after she had put the children to bed, she had sat before a mirror brushing her hair—and thinking—for a full hour. The result was that lamplight shone off her hair, and her face, when Frank walked in and flung the money-filled saddlebags aside, was serene. She looked at him, at his tired face, his sagging shoulders, and the sweat-dust which had dried stiffly on his shirt, and put aside the sewing as she motioned him to a chair and arose without a word to go into the cookshack. He sat, dropped his hat to the floor, gazed at the saddlebags, and when she returned with a big cup of coffee, he smiled at her, speaking for the first time since entering the yard.

'The money's in those bags. Two of the outlaws are on their way to town with Hal Underwood's range-boss—and a man named Carl Holt, the leader of the band, is dead.'

He tasted the coffee, and blinked. It was about one-third straight whiskey. He raised his eyes again, and leaned to put the cup aside. 'I better not finish this; we haven't had anything to eat since yesterday.'

She stared. 'None of you—Tomahawk nor Curtis, either, Frank?'

'No ma'am.'

She pointed. 'Finish it, and just sit there quietly.' She went to the front door, out upon the porch, saw shadowy silhouettes trooping from the direction of the barn, and called softly. 'Curtis—Tomahawk; get cleaned up, then come to the kitchen.'

The men halted out front of the bunkhouse gazing in her direction without saying a word. But after she turned back into the house, Tomahawk sighed. 'It was worth it,' he muttered. 'I don't remember what I did with that damned bar of soap.'

Ella stood in front of Frank, straight and very handsome, hair glistening, strongly-formed, perfect features thoughtful. 'You too,' she said, and smiled at him. 'Get washed, then come to the kitchen . . . Frank?'

He leaned to arise as he said, 'Yes'm?'

'I was worried sick. So was John.'

He pushed himself upright and stood facing her. 'You know what I thought about all the way back— you. How did it go at the cemetery in town?'

'How did it go?'

'Well; I mean, was there anyone out there who looked mean—or anything like that?'

She softly shook her head at him. 'No. There were some cowmen, and a few townsmen. The cowmen removed their hats and stood around. No one said much, but an older man—I don't know his name— afterwards followed us back to the wagon, and gave John a watch. A real one, Frank; a pocket-watch. He was quiet, but so completely understanding.'

Frank said, 'Hal Underwood,' and blinked at her because all that whiskey had suddenly reached his stomach. He turned away. 'I'd better go wash up.'

'I'm glad you're back. I'm glad *all* of you came back, Frank.'

He paused in the hall entry, one hand upon the frame. 'Ella; I was wondering—maybe tomorrow afternoon, if you didn't mind, we could maybe go for a wagon ride over towards the creek. And take a lunch, or something—and maybe talk a little.'

She stood straight, hands clasped in front of her. 'After you've got your sleep,' she murmured, then smiled as she turned to head for the cookshack.

He waited until she was gone before straightening up, facing into the long hallway, concentrating on the door at the far end of it, then casting loose from the wall.

He got out back all right, and filled the basin to wash. He even managed to scrub hard and get clean, but when he was turning back to re-enter the hallway and head for the kitchen, his legs had some difficulty. He felt as though he were very tired, and was climbing a rather steep hill.

Twice he halted. The last time in the parlor by the sofa where she had been sitting when he'd walked in. That was one of his torn shirts she had been sewing.

Out back, he heard the men talking to Ella, heard her soft, gently quiet voice talking back to them, and he told himself he could not possibly let her go away. Not back to Ohio, nor anywhere else. He also told himself that he was drunk, and had to act very un-drunk, so he fixed his eyes upon the cookshack door, straightened up as he had done before, breathed deeply, then pushed off and walked unerringly over where the knob temporarily eluded his hand.

Ella appeared in the doorway, took his arm and led him quietly to the table where the men were already wolfing down food. They did not even look up. Ella eased him down, squeezed his arm as though they shared a secret, then she brought his plate of roast beef, golden-brown potatoes, and more coffee, but

About the Author

Lauran Paine, under his own name and various pseudonyms, has written hundreds of novels. His apprenticeship as a Western writer came about through the years he spent in the livestock trade, rodeos and motion pictures, where he often worked as an extra.

Center Point Publishing
600 Brooks Road ● PO Box 1
Thorndike ME 04986-0001 USA

(207) 568-3717

US & Canada:
1 800 929-9108